SUMMER'S END

It was a sound from hell, something being dragged towards eternal torment; it was a low sound, a last sound; in the silences between, the victim was probably trembling, in mid-collapse. Amy felt that way now. "That can't be an animal."

The scream came again, a long desperate sound which could have been a cat... but only if the cat was suffering the pain of ages... Amy shuddered; was Sarah out there somewhere listening to that?

Then came a worse thought: What if that was Sarah?

Lions

More heart-stopping Nightmares...

NIGHTMARES
SUMMER'S END

Robert Hawks

Lions
An Imprint of HarperCollinsPublishers

First published in the USA in 1994 by Avon Books.
First published in Great Britain in Lions in 1995

1 3 5 7 9 10 8 6 4 2

Lions is an imprint of Collins Children's Books,
a division of HarperCollins Publishers Ltd, 77-85 Fulham
Palace Road, Hammersmith, London W6 8JB

ISBN 0 00 675112 1

Printed and bound in Great Britain by
HarperCollins Manufacturing Ltd, Glasgow.

For Mike and Debi,
just a little more trouble than
anyone possibly needs.

Sleep is lovely, death better still, not to have been born is of course the miracle. . . .

HEINRICH HEINE
1797–1856

prologue

THE HOOKMAN STORY

Patience, Massachusetts, 1959

The August breeze snapped colder than usual, reaching about as if suspicious of the man blocking the moonlight, as if the spirits shuffling the brown oak leaves could read his thoughts. But the breeze tickled the man nonetheless; the wind feared no one.

Nor did the killer.

He moved as a flickering shadow, freeing the lunar light as he shuffled down the hill, toward the half-hidden car on the lovers' lane. He *was* a killer, or soon to be one, soon if he kept his nerve and got them back—got all of them back—for everything they had done to him, or people like him. He was going to show them, trying so hard to show them, all the others, all the kids at school, all the creeps who called him birdman, smelly birdman.

Just because he kept pigeons, just because he had better luck with pigeons than girls they called him birdman, *birdman, birdman, smelly birdman. . . .*

He'd show them. As the killer crept toward the long-finned Chevy parked beneath the oak trees of

1

the lovers' lane, he reached beneath his jacket for the gun, the heavy steel of the pistol. This was his father's weapon, retrieved from the police after the only time Daddy had used it—on himself. Now there would be other targets for the long black-barreled revolver.

And it was going to be easy, so easy, because attached to the end of the barrel was a toy of his own special creation, a silencer made with Daddy's tools from the garage. A rifled steel cylinder to reduce the horrible explosions of the gun to muffled pops.

The killer giggled to himself, just to himself, because laughing would give him away, laughing would make more noise than the gun was going to make when he shot dead the stupid couple making out in the car. . . .

> *"Shelly is your bishie wishie,*
> *Really to be a fishy fishy? . . ."*

Lenore couldn't keep her feet from dancing to the radio as she kissed Mikey, holding herself close to him in the front seat of his dad's Chevy, which was fine because she didn't want to do too much anyway. Just kiss and cuddle and smile at him. Listen to the music.

Mike was a year older than she was, a senior, and he was from Baltimore, here on the island with his family, just as she was there with hers. Lenore was from New York.

Reaching to kiss her, Mike said, "Hey, the rain stopped."

"Yeah," she said, pulling away from his kiss for a moment. "So will you write to me?"

"Sure."

"I mean it. We're only so far away."

2

"I will."

"You could even come up to New York. You could."

"I will. For a ball game, maybe."

"A ball game? Mike!"

He laughed, or started to laugh, but then he saw the look on her face and said, "I'm sorry, I was kidding . . ."

He stopped talking, because Lenore was trembling now, the expression on her face had changed from teasing into terror. She couldn't seem to choke out any words; she didn't have to because he turned.

Toward the window.

Toward the gun.

And he saw it now, despite the windows being a little fogged. There was a guy with a gun standing there, right outside the window, aiming the gun at them. Mike felt his gut cramp. It was like topping out on the ferris wheel, coming down fast, because as Lenore pulled away from him Mike felt his stomach bottoming out and he wondered what it would feel like—

Then the world exploded.

So pleased, so pleased. The killer had tapped the pistol against the glass just once to get their attention before bringing them death. He stepped back for an instant, deciding to shoot the boy first, in the head. Then he would shoot the girl, twice. Once just to wound, so he could watch her, then the *coup de grace*.

Good-bye, creepy teasers who were just like all the others, calling him names, calling him birdman when he couldn't get a date or anything. *I am ready, so ready, and I'm gonna be pleased, so pleased*.

The killer pulled the trigger.

The gun roared and the glass shattered. Too loud, much too loud, he thought. The killer hadn't expected this, not with the silencer, so he squeezed again and again, trying to fire off the shots so he could kill and run away faster than he'd planned. But it was only in this numb moment that the killer realized he was no longer squeezing the trigger because he was no longer *holding* the trigger. *The silencer hadn't worked*! It had jammed the barrel and the gun exploded in his hand *and the gun and his hand were gone*!

His hand was gone!

The killer screamed then. A howl.

The boy and girl in the car were out together now, out the passenger door, running up the road, but the killer was running, too, toward the beach, toward the sea, *because his hand was gone* and he was going to be in so much trouble, so much trouble. This wasn't good, not good, and he was screaming and bleeding so badly now he would probably die, probably have to die, or go to jail. He didn't want to die, didn't want them to say that birdman failed and died, but he didn't want to go to jail. That was worse, that was worse. He didn't want them to be able to laugh at him when he had to go to jail for failing. *For failing*!

There had to be something he could do, *please*, something he could do. And as he charged out into the surf, waist deep, bleeding and screaming in the stinging salty sea, he saw the moon above him and by its light the strange bits of broken crate washing ashore as driftwood. And, as there is no such thing as coincidence in a world filled with static *magick*, he gulped for breath, trying to shove a broken board from his path to drowning, only to be surprised by green-black hands thrusting up from the sea to claw with scaly fingers and pull him down. . . .

I

the island

1

Amy Meyer was always threatening in a loud voice to kill herself in dramatic ways, but on the last Tuesday of June she very nearly succeeded in doing herself in by accident.

It started with her little sister Sarah yapping at her, as always. Tugging on the sleeve of Amy's yellow windbreaker she said, "Come on, we're going to take the picture."

Rolling her eyes at her sister and the world, Amy groaned, brushing black hair from her eyes. Standing alongside her family at the railing of the ferry *Pequod* as it drove through the waters of Terrace Bay, Massachusetts, toward Cyder Island, she took a break from watching the seagulls dive for food and made an appeal to the highest authority. As her younger sister and brother waited, watching the water, Amy said, "Ma, puh-*lease*, this wind is making me look like a mop with ears. How can you take my picture?"

Mrs. Meyer was unimpressed. Shepherding her children was beginning to wear on her; not to mention trying to keep track of the luggage, travel, and lodging arrangements. "You look fine. We're on a boat; it's supposed to be windy."

"Not this windy. I look like some kind of strange mutt dog."

"Relax."

Not likely, thought Amy. Her black hair was beyond control, as always; there was nothing she could do with it.

Amy wasn't happy and wanted to make sure everyone in the known universe knew. "It wouldn't be so bad if Dad was here," she said, which was true. Amy and her father were close; they both loved scary movies and he could figure out a way to have fun in an empty room.

"He'll be out later on."

"Yeah, for a weekend. And maybe a week in August, *if* something doesn't come up. The rest of us are stuck on this stupid island all summer."

"Come on, Amy, you know he'd be here if he could. He loves this part of the country. Your father does have responsibilities."

"Working."

"Yes, *working*. It's not a dirty word."

"This is such a waste," said Amy, looking around for help that wasn't there. "I had things planned for the summer. What about Trish and Margaret and Samantha? What about my friends? This is *my* summer. Who can afford to waste a whole summer?"

"You're fifteen, Amy. You've got a whole lot of summers ahead of you."

"Not with my friends, though."

"I'm sure you'll make some friends on the island." Mrs. Meyer looked around; she had been ready to snap the shot, but now one of the brood was missing. "Where's Katie?"

Katie Meyer was eighteen, the oldest. "Who knows? Who cares?" said Amy. "We wouldn't even be stuck out here if she could stop stealing things."

"That's enough."

"It's true."

Katie reappeared on their side of the deck. Amy saw her mother's frown, but the oldest sister cut her off before she could growl by saying, "I just went to look around."

"Look around for unlocked cars, you mean," sniped Amy.

"Hey," said Katie. "You can just stuff it. I don't care."

"Be quiet, *everybody*," said Mrs. Meyer. "You're making me crazy."

"Why not?" asked Katie, grimacing at Amy. "It runs in the family."

"Why don't they have schools like this thing back in Ohio?" This was from Brian, Amy's brother, who was younger than she but older than Sarah. Amy had nearly forgotten he and Sarah were standing there. He took a break from throwing bread to the birds to ask.

"They do," said Katie. "I just have to go to one at the end of the world. Dad's idea."

"Your father just wants everything to be all right," said Ma. Their mother was not ready to get into all of this again, though, and she cut off discussion by saying, "Kensit School is the best; all the times he's been out this way he's heard nothing but good things. Cyder Island is where we're going to be this summer. *Enough*. This is New England, remember; these people are calm and quiet, polite and I don't think they'll appreciate the constant noise."

"Oh, terrific . . ."

"It's as good as the Vineyard or the Hamptons, let's just take a picture, okay?"

That shut everyone up. They lined up in front of the

railing, Brian in front of Katie and Sarah close beside Amy. Mrs. Meyer stood in front of them, raising the camera to make her adjustments.

Cornered by her mother's picture taking Amy changed the subject. They were nearing the island now, and she asked, "How big is this place, anyway?"

"I don't know," Mrs. Meyer answered.

"Is that the only town?" They could see it now, as the ferry came around to the north side of the island, a small village clustered around the docks and the marina full of pleasure craft.

"That's what the brochure said. *Patience*, Patience, Massachusetts."

"Patience? That's a silly name for a town," said Sarah.

Amy was squinting now; what at first had seemed like a black hill overlooking the town and the sea now looked like a monster, a dinosaur or dragon maybe. "Ma, what's *that?*"

Her mother stared herself. "I don't know."

"Looks like a castle," said Sarah.

"A haunted castle," agreed Brian.

"Castle Cyder."

"Or Castle Patience."

"I don't think it's a castle," said Ma. "I don't know what it is."

"It's big enough," said Amy, starting to walk now down the railing, walking past the people and around the cars toward the back, where the gulls dove and the wake of the propellers churned the water white. She wanted a better look at the black thing overlooking the town. Overlooking *them* now.

It clung to the island's highest point. Compared to the town, its size was almost frightening. If the hill ever collapsed the black dragon would roll down and wipe out everything.

It *was* like a dragon, fearful, with one claw reaching for the town, and a tail dipping out into the sea. What kind of thing was that for a vacation place? This was like rule number one for any monster movie— something weird placed where it wasn't supposed to be and everybody is ignoring it but the hero. . . .

But it wasn't a castle, it wasn't a fortress, and it wasn't a dragon. She could tell as they got closer; it was more like a big black factory. Amy almost felt disappointed. Not scary, just ugly now. The two thrusting columns were smokestacks, not towers; the tail was a dock and pier, and a fence of some kind encircled the place. Whatever it was it seemed a million years old. *What could they possibly make there?*

Suddenly there was a yelp from behind, a woman crying out, "My hat! Hey!" Amy saw something fluttering by her and she dove for it out of instinct, very nearly snagging the hat with her fingertips but at the same time pitching her weight over the railing, throwing off her balance. She was starting to fall.

"*Whoa,*" roared a voice. This came as two strong hands seized Amy from behind and pulled her back. "Easy, girl. Don't drown yourself for a hat."

Amy saw the hat disappear into the bay, then turned to see the man who had saved her. One of the ferry's crew, a young burly type with a graying beard and a brimmed cap stitched with the words *Terrace Bay.* He shook his head in amazement. "More courage than sense, eh?"

"Who are you?"

"Captain Jack."

"You're the Captain?"

"Not so much to be captain of, I know."

"Thanks for saving me."

"My pleasure. Are you going off to that school? On the island?"

"Not me. My stupid sister. I'll probably be running away real soon. How often does this ferry go?"

"Not so often. Once a day, usually. Sometimes twice."

No way, thought Amy. "So what if there's a hurricane or something? How do we get off the island?"

"Well, there're no hurricanes coming, but if there was an emergency the coast guard boys could handle it, I'm sure."

"I don't like this at all," said Amy. "I may have to swim."

"Eleven miles or so, plus sandbars. Can't say I recommend the exercise."

Amy sighed, looking at the island again but seeing nothing but the dragon. *Was it looking back at her*? "So what's this place like?"

"I wouldn't know. I've worked this boat fifteen years and never set foot on so much as the dock."

"What?"

"Saw no need to risk it."

"Risk what?"

Captain Jack was quiet a moment. Then he shrugged. "I saw no need to go against the advice of *my* father, and he said to always keep some water between yourself and Cyder Island."

Rolling her eyes again, Amy said, "Please don't scare me, I see a lot of horror movies and have a very vivid imagination."

Smiling now, Captain Jack said, "Well, I wouldn't worry about it. Most likely just an old sea story. Just something to tell at night."

"Those are the worst kind." Amy started to ask

him some more, but they were approaching the dock now, bells were starting to clang and another crewman called over to Captain Jack and he drifted off back to work.

I definitely do not want to be here, Amy thought as the ferry pulled up to the end of the dock. They were only going there because Katie needed the stamped approval of a summer at the Kensit School.

The Kensit School. A place to straighten out troublemakers, turn lives around in a matter of weeks.

Wonderful.

Amy didn't see how this was fair, the whole family having to go take part in this nonsense just because Katie kept getting busted for shoplifting, partying, etc., but the Kensit School people apparently believed in what they called "A combination of education, discipline, and family support."

For the support side of this, the family needed to be close by, on the island, away from distractions. So they all got to take part in this therapy; everybody had to talk to the shrink. *Double wonderful.* This was why the Meyers were supposed to stay in one of the many beach houses.

Oh, well. The beach house part would probably be cool, anyway. Waking up on the shore, by the ocean. Smelling the salty air, listening to the waves as she drifted off to sleep. Maybe she could even collect some sea shells, find something to salvage.

The ferry docked, the drive ramp was lowered and the Meyers piled back into their rental car, driving off with the other families journeying to the island.

They drove all of a block from the pier, straight to the real estate office, which, Mrs. Meyer was pleased to find, was exactly where it was supposed to be. All the kids piled out of the car to look around while she ducked inside to sign some papers and get the keys and directions to the house Dad leased for them.

This was a surprise. Taking in the whole street in a glance, Amy stuffed her hands in her windbreaker pockets. *Weird.* For a straight New England village the town looked pretty loose; a sign in the butcher shop window announced that they rented videos. The pharmacy was plastered with rock posters, music blaring a little too loudly from the inside; the general store had some pretty hip jackets on sale racks out on the sidewalk. Strangest of all, Ansara Antiques was apparently in the process of being changed into a game arcade; the peeps, whirrs, and explosions of running video games could be heard from inside, although the front window still displayed several old items, including an old spinning wheel and a tremendous ornate bordered mirror. The only sign was hand-lettered and said: "WE'VE GOT RACING SPACE DESTRUCTORS."

"This isn't exactly what the brochure advertised," said Katie, a little confused. Taking the booklet from her, Brian thumbed through, distracting Sarah by explaining how pirates used to live on the island, and how their ghosts probably still did. Sarah was obviously believing none of it; she wanted to go over to the game arcade.

Amy couldn't believe where she was. This was the main street of downtown Patience, Massachusetts, and it looked like the inside of a mall. *Cool.* A man shuffled down the sidewalk, sixty years old or so, wearing a black rain slicker despite the clear weather. He grinned as he passed, saying, "Hey, babes, how goes it?"

Babes? *How goes it*? Amy watched with amazement as the old geezer passed. So much for the staid and quiet New Englanders Ma warned about.

14

There were five or six other people on the street, all of whom seemed to give them a glance—and, in some cases, a grin and a wave. Very friendly, but what sort of a place was this? A T-shirt shack, a jean shop, a video arcade.

"Hey, look at that lady."

This was from Sarah, and they all turned to see what she was talking about. A tired looking homeless woman was pushing a wobbling shopping cart up the center street, passing by the Olde Bookshoppe (and now, it seemed, baseball card shop) ignored by all around her. "What's she doing here?"

"Quiet," said Amy, elbowing her sister to shut up.

The woman was bundled in a heavy coat despite the warm weather, and wore gloves with the fingertips cut off. Leaning forward, she was resting all her weight on the cart, as if the cart was pulling her down the street of its own mind. She was singsonging to herself, "I remember Michael, I remember *Michael*, I know Michael, *Michael*'s never gone 'cause I remember Michael . . ."

The song sounded haunted; a dirge sung in church to ward away evil spirits. *I remember, I remember, I remember Michael.* It reminded her of something and Amy almost shivered. *Creepy.* "Katie, what's that song?"

Her older sister shrugged. "Beats me. Who cares?"

"Grow up."

"I did."

"You know about heart bypass operations? I think you ought to consider a brain bypass."

"You mean like you did?"

"Sarah!"

Katie and Amy both jumped, turning fast. Brian had yelled and moved because as he stood there joking

15

around with Sarah about pirates and the bag lady, both of his little sister's legs had unceremoniously collapsed, her small body crumpling to the sidewalk, jerking about in spasms as her eyes rolled back white and she shuddered and growled.

No, no, not again. . . .

Epilepsy. Amy always remembered with guilt the first time she had seen her little sister go into a seizure; she had burst out laughing. Which wasn't her fault, she told herself again and again, Sarah was just three then, and the attack came so suddenly that she saw it as a game, some funny tantrum Sissy had decided to pull. Only it wasn't, it was an epileptic seizure, and even though Sarah was now on special medicine, the attacks still came—rare, unexpected, but they came.

Brian ran into the real estate office for Ma, while Amy and Katie reacted together, doing their best to keep Sissy from hurting herself, without doing her harm in the process; Katie and Amy had quickly pulled off their jackets and shoved them beneath Sarah's head, so she wasn't jerking it back into the concrete of the sidewalk. Reacting to a seizure wasn't like in the movies, you weren't supposed to grab the person and shove a stick between her teeth or anything, you just watched and tried not to let her ram into anything, or bang her head on the sidewalk.

Ma was outside with Brian then, but it was mostly over; Sarah was calm now, unconscious but soon to wake up; her arms were scraped but fortunately she hadn't banged the back of her head too badly; the jackets helped.

Ma didn't freak, she stayed controlled and serious. "Stand back, Amy," she said, bending down with Katie. They were waiting for Sarah to open her eyes. Epilepsy was like an electrical short circuit in the brain, Amy knew; something popped and the person lost control for a few moments, but there was also the problem of waking up after the seizure, realizing how helpless and out of control you had been, and suddenly being overwhelmed; when Sarah started to realize what the seizures were she had cried a lot afterward, from embarrassment.

"Come on," Amy said to Brian, pulling him back as Sarah came around. Right or wrong, the best thing for them to do since Sarah was all right was to ignore it, let Ma and Katie calm her down, let Ma murmur about how important it was for Sarah to take her medicine.

Pulling her brother by the arm, Amy looked around some more while the family regrouped. She listened to the Guns n' Roses CD blaring from the pharmacy.

This place was wild, definitely not the dead boring town she'd been afraid of. Amy had to admit it. Left to find the remedial counseling school for her goofy older sister, Dad had come through again. . . .

Things islanders are supposed to learn:

Before Socrates drank the hemlock, before the Aztecs sacrificed their first living heart, before Atlantis fell, something terrible happened, something monstrous, something accidental. Life thrives on future moments; death sulks about the past. For every birthright on earth there is a curse somewhere in the world, and someone more than willing to pass it along. Creatures of tainted existence feed, but are always ravenous. Loosed but cursed, they may not comprehend but they remember everything.

Things islanders have learned instead:

The baddest, most evil monster in the world can't ride a skateboard. . . .

2

Mrs. Meyer located the house on Crescent Road easily enough, taking only about fifteen minutes and one wrong turn. On the drive they passed several unattended lawns and two loud parties. Beating the others to the front porch, Amy was pleased to see it was a nice enough place, positioned between the winding road and the sandy shoreline. There were three bedrooms, wood floors, a fireplace, and a four-foot, stone retaining wall dividing the house lot from the actual beach.

The first order of business was to make sure Sarah was all right and had taken her medicine. Next came the unloading of the car and the unpacking of the bags. Amy's initial unpacking consisted of tossing her suitcase on the lower bunk of the room she and Sarah were being forced to share. Which wasn't fair, since Brian got his own room. Because of her problems, Katie was required to live in a dorm on the school grounds. Which was fine with Amy, since it made for less hassles and more room for the rest of them.

They were there all of an hour before her mother established a list of chores that needed to be done, but Amy wasn't the only one putting them off. Rushing by on his way through the living room, her brother

Brian almost plowed Amy right over. "Hey," she said. "Where are you going?"

"Outside," he answered. "Carlos is waiting for me."

"Who?" Amy peeked outside; there was a pale, brown-haired boy standing outside.

"Carlos. He's an islander."

"An island what?"

"And *islander*. He lives here."

"And that makes him an island person?"

"Islanders are people who are born on the island," explained Ma, coming out of the back room for another load. "Who's the islander?"

"Brian's new friend," said Sarah, making her observation from her seat before the television set. She was talking again, which was good.

"That's nice." Ma waved through the screen door.

"How did you make a friend already?" Amy was jealous.

Brian shrugged. "He was outside and said hello. We're going to do water balloons."

"And drop them on who? There's nobody here."

"Nah, there's lots of people here. You'll see."

Amy nodded, feeling tired. "Oh, yeah. Sounds major."

Brian went outside. Kicking around the house looking for something to do that wouldn't leave her bored to screams, Amy found her mother in one of the back bedrooms, moving clothes from suitcases to dressers. "Can I walk back into town?"

"Not right now, help me get straightened around."

"Ma, *puh*-lease . . ."

"The curtains on your and Sarah's room are missing. I'll pick up some, but in the meantime I pulled a sheet out of the linen and hung it up there."

"Terrific, very classy. So can I walk into town and buy some curtains?"

"We'll go in a little while. Why don't you go out and look at the beach?"

"I've seen sand already."

"Then look at the ocean."

"Same thing."

"You could start the grocery list."

"You've already got a grocery list."

"So make it longer."

"Why? I'll just have to help put it all away."

"Amy, please don't make me throw you into the ocean."

"I just want to see what this place is like."

Her mother looked out the window. "There's an old shed back there. Who knows what might be inside? Money, jewels, horrible dead bodies . . ."

Curious but doubtful, Amy frowned and peeked around her mother's shoulder. "Probably nothing but gardening stuff."

"So dig up the garden. See who's buried in it."

"Funny."

Amy went back out to the living room, where Sarah sat in front of a snowy television, trying to watch something. "What show is that?" asked Amy.

"I don't know, I can't see it right," said Sarah. "The picture's all messed up. There must be something wrong with the cable."

Amy laughed. "Cable? There's no cable on this island. That's just regular television."

"What?"

"Off the antenna. You know, through the air?"

Sarah didn't understand, and Amy tried to explain it to her. She looked around the furnishings of the living room for some rabbit ears or something, and found some wires connected to the back of the set.

They led to a wall outlet and outside, up to the roof presumably. "I'll fix it," said Amy, making an instant decision. She didn't have anything else better to do. Besides, she wasn't afraid of heights.

Come to think of it, she wasn't afraid of much.

Amy prowled around the outside of the house. There was an old and weathered wooden ladder beside the shed, not easy to lift and harder to carry, but Amy managed to drag it over to the house. Passing one of the windows she saw her mother inside, still unpacking things.

Not the person she wanted to see her crawling up on the roof. Amy had to be quiet about it, take things easy.

Okay. Taking a deep breath she pulled and lifted, gently pushing the ladder up against the side of the wall. It slumped into place with an easy but comforting thud, the feet of the ladder secure and not wobbling.

She tested the first rung by stepping up on it, first with one foot, then both. The ladder took her full weight with no problems. Amy started climbing, slow, easy, and got up to the roof. It was high, but no worse than trees she used to climb as a kid. Besides, she'd snuck up to the school roof back home with some friends before. It was pretty cool, though, this view she had earned for herself. King of the Hill. King of the house, really.

She walked quietly, not wanting her mother to come running outside and have a nervous breakdown. And why? It wasn't as if she was going to run around up here, trying to smash down through the roof shingles, all she was doing was fixing an antenna.

She found that easily enough, and it had fallen over. The base was bent, maybe from a high wind, and the metal tubing at the top was tangled in some wires coming from the light pole. That was probably what was messing up the reception.

"Hey! Stop! On the roof! Stop!"

Amy was walking over to the antenna when she heard this, and she did stop, blinking and looking around. Who was yelling?

Down below and toward the shoreline. There was a guy running up from the beach, just a little older than she was, waving his arms and calling up to her. "Don't move. Don't touch anything."

Amy waved back at him to shut up, stop yelling. What was he trying to do? Get her nailed? Mom would go nuts. Better to just fix the antenna and get down.

Except the crazy guy yelled again. "No, hey! Don't move. Don't touch anything!"

He was down beside the house now and Amy shook a fist at him. "What? Why? Could you keep it down?"

"Just stop, okay? Okay?" Uninvited, he ran around the house and clumped his way quickly up the ladder and onto the roof with her. "Freeze. Don't move."

"Why?"

"Because I don't want you to die."

"What?"

Walking over to where she was, stepping easy to avoid slipping on the roof shingles, he crept over to where she was and pointed out the problem. "That antenna's lying up against the power lines. Didn't you see that? If you touch it you'll fry."

This guy was cute, tall with blond hair and freckles, but was he trying to make her look like an idiot? "What are you talking about?"

"You'll ground yourself. That's how electricity works, the power wants the earth. I know all about this stuff. You touch that antenna and the electricity will go from the wire to the antenna to you. From you to the ground and pop, you're fried."

"You're kidding."

He shook his head.

Amy took a long moment to consider this. "Oh my God," she said then, stepping back as if the thing was a poisonous snake, which she guessed it was.

The guy jumped to keep her from going too far. "Easy! Don't fall off the roof," he said. "Just don't touch the antenna."

"Oh, no."

"Do you always just walk around up here?" He seemed impressed. His face brightened as he looked at her and Amy wondered why.

She shrugged. "I was trying to fix Sarah's TV."

"Sarah?"

"My little sister. Her show's all snowy and fuzzy."

"And you're not scared to crawl up on roofs?"

"Why? You're not."

"No, but—"

"If you say 'but I'm a guy' we'll find out real quick how well you fly."

He grinned at that. "Oops. Sorry. I'm Travis." He held out his hand for a shake.

A *shake*? Amy frowned at his hand. She was about to tell him her name, but Ma did it for her, calling now from below. "Amy? What's going on? What are you doing up there?"

Amy looked at Travis and then down at her mother. "I'm trying to get this goofy guy off our house."

"What?" Multiple reactions, from both her mother below and the guy up on the roof with her.

Which was exactly what Amy was looking for. So now she called down. "This is Travis."

24

Still craning her neck to look up at them, Mrs. Meyer nodded. "Well, since you're up there, can you see Katie around anywhere?"

Amy looked around and then shook her head. "No."

"It's almost two o'clock and I'm supposed to take her over to orientation. She's enrolled tomorrow."

"Want me to walk into town and see if she's there?"

"Not right now, Amy. Please . . ." Mrs. Meyer disappeared back inside.

Travis seemed amused by all of this, his face bright, and again Amy wondered why. Was he so bored that this represented great entertainment to him? Terrific, so wonderful. She said, "Let's get down, okay? I don't want to fix the antenna anymore. I have suddenly lost all interest in electronic repair."

They climbed down and Travis helped her move the ladder. Travis asked, "So, Amy, my electrician friend, are you going to Kensit?"

Amy frowned. "No. Are you? Or are you one of these islanders I heard about?"

Travis shook his head. "Nah, my mom and dad just got jobs there this summer; teachers."

"So you're an islander now, huh?"

"Nope. Can't be an islander unless you're born here. That's the rule. After the summer I'm getting sent off to boarding school. A different one, I mean."

"Boarding school? Really? Where?"

"New Hampshire."

"Sounds dull."

"It's okay, I went there last year."

"Is it a military school or something?"

"No, but I was in one of those once. Got kicked out after four weeks for not making my bed properly."

Amy nodded. "So, you're loud, a know-it-all, and a slob. At least I know all your faults."

"Oh, no. I've got plenty more."

"I'll bet you do. So what are you, on beach house patrol today? Sent out to keep people from killing themselves on the roofs and such?"

"Nah, that's just my hobby. Actually, I was walking up the beach to see if Wally's there."

"Wally?"

"Wally's a fisherman. Used to be, anyway. He's definitely an islander. I met him the other day. Kind of a kook, but he's all right. Wants to be a pirate. He's got an eye patch, he lives on this cool boat, and he's got lots of good stories. Want to come?"

"And listen to fish stories from a one-eyed pirate?"

"He's got two eyes. He just likes to wear the patch."

"I don't think so."

Travis looked disappointed, but he said, "Maybe I'll stop by later. See if you're fried yet."

Amy answered with a casual shrug. "Whatever works."

She watched him go; he was all right. She didn't want to marry him or anything, but he was all right. Maybe he would come back, or she might see him around. After all, it was a small island. . . .

After her orientation, the family picked up Katie so they could all eat dinner together. It would be the last time before the weekend, since once enrolled Katie was supposed to live on the school grounds.

They were eating at a seafood place called Tucker's in the village. The waitress was really casual, but she got the order right despite seeming annoyed to even be there. Katie hated her new school already. "This whole town is goofy," she said.

"Goofy?" Mrs. Meyer had gone with her daughter and didn't think the place was so bad.

"Yeah, they're all wise guys. They don't seem like teachers; they don't take anything seriously."

"Maybe they're just giving you a little of your own back," said Ma.

"Besides, the place gives me the creeps," she said. "It's right on the other side of that old cannery. God knows what lives in there."

"Cannery?" asked Amy.

"That's your dragon," explained Ma. "It's an old fish cannery."

"Color me gone," said Katie. "The place is a loony bin."

As always, Katie was trying to lay on the guilt. Amy talked into her plate. "If you die can I have your CDs?"

"No."

Sarah was eating a cheeseburger since she didn't like fish, and she said to Katie, "You'll be okay, Katie."

Katie sighed. "At least somebody cares."

For a moment Amy did feel sorry for her sister. She was remembering the creepy feeling she had looking up at the dragon—*a fish cannery?*—and Katie's feeling toward the Kensit School was probably Amy's feeling toward Cyder Island, only multiplied a hundred times or so.

Oh, well. Katie brought it on herself, Amy thought. She brought it on all of them.

The evening wore down; Amy goofed around with Sarah a while, trying to fix her hair up properly and then working on her own. A hopeless task. Finally Amy decided to just go to bed; she was surprised at how tired she was. Probably just boredom, although she was thinking again about Travis, the rooftop electrical genius. It was a sarcastic thought, but he was cute, and probably had kept her from getting zapped off the roof.

She never even realized she'd fallen asleep until she awoke in the dark room. A rustling sound stirred her up and she realized the bedsheet making up for the missing curtains had slipped from the window frame. *Wonderful.* The neatness freak inside of her said to get up and rehang it, and she nearly rose, but that was when another strange voice inside her head emerged, a sudden, freaky, pleading voice begging *stop!*

Amy actually shivered, wondering if maybe she was still sleeping, simply dreaming, because she had never in her entire life been so suddenly overcome by fear. Except in a nightmare. This chill felt like the terror of a nightmare.

Because in that instant she knew she was being watched. Not suspected, not thought, not wondered, she *knew*.

Just a few feet away, some terrible face was pressed tight against the glass, staring at her and Sarah. Amy felt this for a fact, she could see it in her mind's eye, and her blood was running cold.

What face? Who was it? An ax murderer? Some demented serial killer? Some island hopping madman?

Stupid. Just turn and look, clear the image.

No. Someone was there. The dementia felt so real, so certain, it was as if somehow her mind and that of the person watching her were connected.

If Amy turned she was sure to see him, and that would be that. That would be it.

She fought the urge. Trembling, psyching herself out, Amy chewed on her lip and clawed at the blankets, wondering what she could do, how she could

protect herself if she looked and there was some were-
wolf or monster or some alien space creature standing
there, studying her.

This was crazy. Her heart was pounding so hard it
might burst, would burst, *had* to burst, and Amy felt
her muscles so tight she couldn't turn, couldn't look
across the room, it couldn't be done; the movement
was impossible.

She looked.

The window was empty.

Just the night and the moonlight, the hilltop silhouette of the cannery's towers and the distant beach.

Soaked in sudden sweat, Amy got up and walked
over to the window. Had she been sleeping? How
much of all that was a nightmare?

There was somebody out there, or at least she thought
she saw somebody, but whoever it was stood down on
the beach, near the breakwater, silhouetted against the
ocean surf. A beachcomber, probably. But that struck
Amy as odd. Why would anybody be down there at
this hour? It was pretty late. And when she closed her
eyes to wipe away the sleep, he was gone. . . .

Something else islanders are required to know: The philosophers were wrong: words may be unwritten, existences can be dissolved as sugar in water, Merlin did live his life backwards.

Antonia is a name no one recalls; the true mentor of Michaelangelo, and a much better artist. Antonia was taken, and all his creations, all his masterworks, all his effect on his world was undone. The memory of mankind has many scars which cannot heal. Islanders should know this; like the Great Master, they remember all.

Unlike the Great Master, they just don't care as much as they should.

Some things islanders do care about:
MTV, pizza, and basketball.

3

The next morning was as bright and sunny as the morning breakfast scene with the good wholesome family, which was just about enough to make Amy gag. Mrs. Meyer made French toast, an act that struck Amy as a major world event. "Alert CNN," she said, dragging herself in her bathrobe into the kitchen. "Since when do you cook in the morning?"

"Since your sister isn't around to do it," said Mom, bringing food over from the stove.

"She never did it before half the time."

"Get dressed."

Amy did. When she got back to the kitchen Sarah and Brian were already eating and her mother was setting down a plate for her. "Enjoy, but don't get used to this," she said. "I'm usually too busy for French toast."

"You're usually too busy for cornflakes."

Her mother ignored that, saying, "Still, it's really nice here. Don't you think so? I've got the windows open; I love that smell off of the ocean."

"I think that's an oil spill."

Sitting down to eat, Mrs. Meyer lifted her fork and shook her head dramatically. "Amy, Amy. Don't you ever think of the glass as half-full?"

"Sure. My life is half-full. Half-full of something . . ."

Mrs. Meyer gave a motherly scowl but Sarah and Brian both laughed. They all ate for a while until Amy said, "I'm going to go for a walk this morning, okay? Down the beach, into town?"

"We're going later if you want a ride."

"Nah, I want to look around."

"Look around for that boy, maybe," teased Sarah.

"Just look around, thank you very much."

After breakfast Amy helped clean up and load the dishwasher, then she watched from the front porch as the whole crew piled into the car, her brother and sister arguing over who got to ride in the front seat with Mom; neither did. Amy congratulated herself on her wisdom for skipping that nonsense. Instead she went down to the beach, to look around for the footsteps of the person she had seen standing there in the night.

Which was stupid, what with the tide and all that. Any tracks would have been washed clear almost right away. Silly.

But who could it have been? Who would be wandering around out there in the middle of the night? Could it have been Travis, the great rooftop electrical genius? Maybe he came around looking for her. She envisioned him peering in her window. Was he the Peeping Tom sort?

Not likely. It could have been almost anybody, she supposed. After all, it wasn't a private beach or anything.

So Amy wandered a while, getting some exercise, catching some rays and smelling the salty sea air. She walked along the beach—it was either that or the road beyond the berm, and at least here she had the lonely surf to keep her company. Sea birds dived for their snacks just offshore, and the occasional dead fish shared the sand with shells and rocks.

Way out on the horizon now a big boat—*a ship, come on, get it right, you're living on an island now*—was headed somewhere out to sea. Maybe it was going to Europe, or to Africa. Or down to the Bahamas. Too bad she couldn't flag them down for a ride.

Back on shore, something was up ahead, just off the beach. How far had she wandered? A ways, anyway. Amy frowned, walking closer, fascinated by what she saw.

A good forty feet inland from the beach sat a large, aging fishing boat, buried in sand up to where the waterline would be, had the ship been in the water. Another thirty feet inland from the ship was a wrecked house, splintered wood and brick on a shattered concrete foundation, broken pipes and half an interior wall reaching up; it looked a lot like what their rental house might resemble if a bomb were detonated inside.

Very strange, Amy thought as she walked closer. A tattered flag ruffled on the mast of the grounded ship, the only sound besides the surf. The weathered, faded name on the boat's bow read *TANGERINE 2.*

"Bright morning."

Amy jumped, turning toward the sudden voice. An old man in a grungy, black, stocking cap and an eye patch across his right eye was walking up behind her; obviously he had been on the other side of the ship, hidden from her view. Was he the one she had seen on the beach the night before? What about him? Had he been peeking in her window?

"I say it's a bright morning. So what do you think?"

Amy shivered, saying nothing; the old man scratched at the fleshy folds in his face with red stubby fingers. Grunting toward the scene she was watching—the boat and the house—the old guy explained: "Beached in 1977; same storm that wrecked the house and killed my three dogs. Beautiful dogs, show animals. Sea rose up and drowned them all. Didn't seem much point in cleaning up after all that. Sorry if it bugs you."

"Bugs me?"

"You know, makes you upset?"

"I'm not upset." Remembering what she had heard the day before, Amy asked, "Are you Wally?"

The man grinned. "Yeah, Wally McFlint. What are you, a mind reader? I hope not."

"This guy told me about you yesterday. Travis."

Wally nodded. "I know Travis. He was around here yesterday again."

"He says you're an islander."

"As I am. Travis has an eye for the ladies, I see."

Amy felt herself blush a bit. Not so much. "*Tangerine 2*," she said, admiring the boat. "Why *Tangerine*?"

"I like tangerines."

"Oh. So what happened to *Tangerine 1*?"

"Well, now, I'll answer you that. She's about twenty miles east of here, under three hundred feet of water and guarded by the ghost of an old friend of mine who had the misfortune of getting his leg busted and pinned just as the weather went all to hell. I'd say something right and proper like it should have been me, but I'm glad it was him."

"What?" Amy almost took a step back.

"My buddy Harry Brooks, may he rest in peace. Or burn in hell; I don't suppose with Harry it would make much difference. Might keep the devil's days interesting."

"When did that happen?"

"Almost sixty-four years now, I guess."

"Sixty-four years?"

The sailor hesitated. "Yeah. So?"

Amy shook her head. "You don't look that old."

He frowned. "I don't really like tourists."

"Sorry." Amy felt herself staring. The man, Wally, looked away, saying, "I can't catch a break with the sea. That's why I stay away from her now."

"Stay away from her? You live on a boat on the beach."

"Yeah, well, this is as far away as I can pull myself."

"Travis said your eye patch wasn't for real."

Grinning, Wally leaned in close and lifted it, exposing his hidden eye and saying, "No, but it keeps the tourists happy when they see me. Fits the image. People buy me drinks." His harsh breath almost knocked her over, and Amy turned away, immediately embarrassed. *Onions!* Wally caught her reaction and laughed. "Hah! Don't let me breathe you away, missy, just keep me downwind. Just another of my bad habits."

"Sorry."

"Don't you be sorry. Old Cyder Island tale, eat your wild onions."

"Why?"

"Wouldn't *you* like to know?"

"What?"

Old Wally laughed, saying only, "Yeah, wouldn't you like to know . . ."

Amy nodded, backing away and leaving as quickly as she could and walking further up the beach, but she didn't find Travis. Instead, a mile or so beyond the wreck of the boat and house, outside of the next bungalo up the beach she lucked into meeting a couple of girls her age; they both wore sunglasses and cutoff jeans. One was a very tall girl with long black hair, the other was a frizzy-haired blond whom Amy thought she recognized.

Their attention apparently divided between the stereo headphones they were wearing and the magazines in their laps. They were kicked back in a pair of beach chairs watching over—baby-sitting—a pair of twin boys, seven years old or so, who were supposedly building a sand castle, but who seemed more determined to dig some huge ditch. Naturally, and much to their amazement, it kept filling with water.

But Amy kept staring at the blond girl. She ventured closer. *Yeah*, she thought, *it looked like her. Maybe . . . maybe it was her. . . .*

Why not ask? "Hey," said Amy, "I don't want to bother you guys, but didn't I see you get eaten by a giant leech?"

The girl looked up. "That was a giant slug," she said, pulling off her headphones. "You know what a slug is?"

"No."

"Just a homeless snail. I got away from the leeches, both times."

Breaking out into a grin, Amy said, "So you are Liz Conner? The Liz Conner? From the movies?"

"I was in three movies. I'm going to be in another."

"Another leech movie?"

The girl grimaced. "No, it's not another leech movie. It's a real movie, with guys, and cars, and jokes, and nobody gets their blood sucked out. Who are you?"

"I'm nobody."

"What?"

"I mean I'm Amy Meyer. I'm nobody special, I'm just here, I'm . . ."

"So what are you? Inmate or guard?"

36

"I'm sorry . . ." Amy didn't understand.

Clicking off her tape deck, Liz tilted her head some. "I mean, are you an inmate or a guard? Are you getting that Kensit treatment?"

Amy was a little surprised by the question. "No. I thought all the students there had to stay on the campus."

"Not necessarily. They run off a lot. You'll see them around."

"See them? I live with one."

"Most of us do. Mine's my sister."

"Really? Your sister has to go to Kensit? That's so wild."

"Why?"

"Well, because . . . you're a movie star."

Liz rolled her eyes. "I'm not a movie star; I've only been in three very stupid movies, and all three of them were made by my Uncle LeRoy. I might be in a good movie this fall, though. Unless this girl from a soap opera gets the part instead."

"You've had big parts."

"No way. In every one I spent the whole time chasing bugs. Some career." Liz offered the third beach chair and introduced her friend. "This is Marcia Ratner—she's the Rat. Why don't you park for a while?"

"Okay." Amy sat down and answered; Rat waved from underneath her headphones, saying nothing, and Liz said, "Nice to meet you, Amy M."

Her head spinning a little, Amy said, "I can't believe I'm sitting here talking to you. I loved those movies. You've got the greatest scream . . ."

Shrugging, Liz said, "They were all right. Kind of gross. It's weird to sit and eat popcorn and watch yourself die. I probably shouldn't make so many Kensit

School jokes. A few more leech movies and I'll be there myself."

"Really?" Amy watched the twins dig for a minute. "Are those your brothers?"

"No, not Rat's either, but we're drafted. Baby-sitting for the neighbors."

"You have to baby-sit?"

"You've gotta relax, Amy M. My Uncle LeRoy makes cheap drive-in slasher movies and I work for him cheap so I can go to college later."

Amy nodded, accepting that. "It's just so weird."

"Everything is weird on Cyder Island; get used to it. Here, these are the Rudnick twins, Taylor and Tyler. T and T, how stupid. If I had twins I'd give one away."

"You wouldn't."

"Maybe not, but at least I'd name them sensibly. Call one Tom and the other Jerry."

"No way."

"How about Zachary and Ulysses?"

Amy laughed. "That's workable."

"I'm too young to have kids anyway."

"I should think so."

"Come to think of it, I'm too young to be stuck baby-sitting. I should be out on the prowl."

That made Amy smile. "On the prowl?"

"Sure. You interested?" Liz took off her sunglasses. "We've got the lowdown on all the hot guys stuck on the island with us. Let us keep you straight."

"Keep me what?"

"Goofus-proof. Me and Rat can save you a lot of time sorting the riff from the raff, you know? Avoid the losers, save valuable time and effort."

"I'll keep that in mind."

Rat leaned forward, speaking now for the first time. "What do you want out of life, anyway?"

38

Amy stared at Rat a long moment before she realized she was joking; all three started laughing at the same time. Amy shrugged. "I already met somebody. One somebody, anyway."

Rat leaned back in her chair. "So what's up?"

"Not so much." Amy told them about her rooftop confrontation with Travis. Liz pretended to swoon. "Oh, and he's a hero and everything."

"He's not a hero, I'm an idiot."

Slipping her sunglasses back on, Liz said, "There are worse ways to start summer than falling in love."

"I'm not falling in love."

"So you're falling in like, what's the difference?"

Rat said, "We're burning down the beach tonight. You ought to come on down."

"You'll have to explain that one."

Liz did. "Big bonfire—guys, music, dancing, flirting, you name it. Even a little making out in dark shadows if you've got the nerve." Holding up her magazine Liz said, "According to these know-it-all astrologers the full moon isn't until Saturday night. Gonna be lots of shadows . . ."

This surprised Amy; a party? Lots of others her age? This vacation was turning out to be greater than anything she would have thought possible—Katie would be out of her hair, not mocking her all the time, the town was like a mall, there were lots of other kids and parties, and here she was on the first day out going to hang out with the star of some of her favorite horror movies.

So there were one or two strange things walking around in the night. Big deal. *This was going to be the best vacation of her life. . . .*

The Great Master has begun to question the sanity of His Own Great Mind, because control has begun to slip from Him. Every islander supposedly knows the rules: stay your life, hold the silence, live for the summers when the world you can't touch comes to you.

Remember, us and them, us and them, islanders and off-islanders. And remember the punishments. Consumption. To be absorbed is to be one with Him, not truly extinguished, simply undone and taken, and no hell could be worse than that.

Islanders are supposed to be special. . . .

Except—for some not easily explained reason—His legion of disciples have discovered a frightening new religion: rock-and-roll music. . . .

4

After they left the beach—escorting Taylor and Tyler Rudnick home—Liz and Rat followed Amy back to the beach house. On the way Amy got another surprise; Rat wanted to teach kindergarten, which explained her tolerance for the Rudnick twins. She thought baby-sitting was good practice for hearing a thousand and one questions and watching little kids run around like maniacs.

Liz, of course, was working on being a movie star, and that was something Amy could identify with, loving horror movies as she did. They discussed guys a while, discovering one more thing they had in common: none of them had a boyfriend, although Rat did once, a greasy-haired guy named Tony who became a junior varsity football player and had since moved his romantic sights to cheerleaders. Rat didn't seem to care; she had stuff other than guys on her mind, but it sounded like Liz seldom thought of anything else. Amy figured she was somewhere in the middle.

Up at the bungalow Sarah was chattering around the house, playing squirrel. Liz and Rat laughed; Sarah was being silly, but it was okay; there were people over and she wanted attention and was getting it.

Amy went into the kitchen to find Ma, and did; she had just stuck a large frozen pizza into the oven and came out to say hello, frowning a bit at Liz, recognizing her from somewhere, but not realizing it was from the movies Amy watched endlessly on the VCR. "I don't know your parents, do I?"

"No, just my Uncle LeRoy."

"What?"

Amy told the story, and Ma was properly impressed. "Hey, I'll bet that's a lot of fun."

"It's okay."

Sarah interrupted, not as impressed and trying to get on with her own version of life. She said, "Whatever, just don't let any cats in here. Cats hate squirrels and I'd hate to see a cat in here."

"No problem," said Amy.

"My squirrel husband will be home in a little while, you know."

Rat frowned. "Your squirrel husband?"

"Yes. He's at the store right now buying acorns."

"Right."

Grabbing a magazine from the coffee table, Rat settled back down and asked Liz, "So, what are we going to do?"

"Get myself one of those squirrel husbands."

"Right."

They all shared the frozen pizza and as they ate Amy told her mother about the beach party that night. Ma thought that sounded good, but unfortunately so did Sarah, who chimed in immediately. "Can I go? Can I go?"

Amy heard her own bells then; alarm bells in her brain. "No way."

"Please."

Trying to con Sarah off, Amy said, "It's not that kind of a party."

"What kind?"

"A little kid kind."

Sarah was offended. "I'm not a little kid."

Rat agreed, saying, "I wouldn't want to be accused of corrupting a squirrel."

"I'm only as little as I act—Ma says."

Amy shot a look at her mother, who had to confess. "That is what I say."

"She can't come out—it'll be dark."

"I don't really want you wandering around in the dark, either, Amy."

Embarrassed, Amy said, "Ma, *puh*-lease!"

"All right, all right, go. And, Sarah, you stay here with me and Brian." Ma waved her off; Liz and Rat decided to hang around and wait on her, then stop by their own houses on the way. Amy grabbed a shower and was getting dressed when Rat said, "I wish my mom was like yours. I think she's having a nervous breakdown on the installment plan. The woman is so uptight she doesn't brush her teeth—she sends them out to be dry-cleaned."

Amy shrugged. "Ma's all right."

"What about your dad?"

"He's super cool, but won't be here for a while. He's got a lot of work back home."

Ready to go, Amy led the way out the side door and they started up the beach in the direction Travis had come from that first day. They stopped at Liz's, and Rat ran across the way to her own house, coming back showered but not looking very much different. "Rat's not big on fashion," said Liz, who apparently was. Rat explained the bag she was carrying. "I've got to stop off on the way at the Rudnick place—the twins? My mother told *their* mother she had a stack of romance books, so I get to play delivery girl."

They talked all the way, and in between her "Not much further," assertions Liz traded more stories. Amy found out Liz and her family were from Philadelphia, Pennsylvania and always spent summers at some beach house somewhere. "Key West, Long Island, Charleston; one year we even spent three weeks in Scotland."

"Scotland? Really?"

"Yeah."

"That must have been cool."

"Only for my parents. They live for this stuff."

"And you're doing another movie in the fall?"

"Yeah, maybe. If the girl from the soap opera doesn't get the part over me—we both had to go read at an audition. Her name's Sasha, which is supposed to be cool except Sasha is a guy's name in Russian. I hope I get the part because it's a really good script. Nobody gets killed."

"Hang on a second," said Rat then, climbing the back berm toward a house; Amy and Liz followed while Rat banged on the back screen door so hard they both cringed. "Gotta be heard," Rat said.

Amy watched. Mrs. Rudnick answered, smiling, "Hey, guys."

"Bag from Mom," said Rat, passing it over.

"This is Amy Meyer," said Liz, making the introductions. "Her family is up the beach from you, between us. Where's the twins? Amy's got a little brother and sister, they'd probably get along."

Mrs. Rudnick smiled. "What?"

"The twins, they're quiet tonight. Usually they come running out to say hi at least. They should meet Amy's brother and sister."

"Twins?"

"Taylor and Tyler."

44

Mrs. Rudnick pulled one of the paperbacks from the bag and shrugged, as if she didn't have the slightest idea what Liz was talking about. So Rat pushed it: "Can I say hi?"

"Hi?"

"To the boys."

"Is that where you guys are going?" Mrs. Rudnick smiled.

Amy looked at her two friends; all were confused now, and Liz said, "We meant your boys, the twins."

Now the woman in the doorway acted genuinely surprised. "My boys?"

"Yeah, your kids."

The woman laughed now, shaking her head and backing into the house. "Come on, guys, you know I don't have any kids . . ."

They walked on toward the party, and even though Amy didn't fully understand what was going on, Liz and Rat wouldn't let it go. Rat was laying it all out. "And their mother says they aren't home. Worse. Says they were never home, that we've got something all mixed up because there were never any Rudnick twins. It must all be in our heads."

"It isn't in my head," said Liz. "I know the inside of my head pretty well."

Amy nodded.

"She says she doesn't have any kids! Their own mother! Amy, you saw them. You know the Rudnick twins were real kids."

Amy shrugged. "I saw kids. Maybe you guys got the names wrong. Maybe that wasn't their mom."

"We baby-sat for them all week, I've been in their house. God, I hope she didn't murder them or something."

"Murder them?"

"Yeah," said Liz, considering it all, touching Rat's arm as she jumped in and thought it through. "This is too weird. Maybe we're dreaming; is this a dream?"

"You guys said we were going to a party."

"We are going to a party," said Rat. "We're just wondering if maybe we're also going crazy."

Liz looked around. "You believe us, don't you?"

"Yeah. Maybe."

"Maybe?"

"Well," said Amy. "This is like the number one thing in a horror movie, and you have been in some horror movies. Maybe you're playing a game with me or something."

"Us? What are you talking about?"

"The number one thing in any horror movie is when everybody thinks the hero is crazy, even though we know the hero is right."

"Do you think she killed her kids?" asked Rat. "Or sold them to somebody? I read about that, once."

Amy shrugged. "I don't know. How does a person know what to believe? I mean, do you always believe what you see, what you hear?"

Liz said, "My Uncle LeRoy says never believe your own lying eyes . . ."

The party was on Kelly's beach, said Liz as they got closer. "Kelly's an islander, but she's all right, I guess. A little weird. Her breath stinks, but her mom and dad are buying the food and stuff, so who cares?"

You didn't knock on the door of a beach party, Amy discovered; you just wandered up on it. It wasn't far from the fish cannery pier, and from here the sleeping dragon of the dead factory seemed close enough to touch. Close enough to throw rocks at, anyway; a lot of the windows were broken.

At first the crowd of kids seemed more a mob than a party, the fire wasn't even going yet but that changed soon enough. The sun was setting, a flame sparked and fire reached for the sky and soon hot dogs and burgers were cooking. Amy didn't see any adult-chaperone types, but there was a big dark house overlooking the beach, all the lights out, and she supposed some might be casually watching from up there. There was also the cannery. Was anyone watching from there, from the blackness? "Come on," said Liz, "let's see who's doing what to whom."

They walked around, checking things out. There were a surprising number of kids at the beach party; there were about four different sources of music, stereos and tape decks blaring, a volleyball game going, and at least a dozen conversations. "This is all right."

Grinning, Liz said, "What did you expect? This is a resort island-prison, we've got the best of the worst worlds. Look, there she is."

"Who?"

"Kelly, this is her party."

"Where do you know her from?"

"Liz insists on knowing everybody," said Rat.

They watched Kelly walking around. She was a terribly nervous redhead with wild hair and thick glasses, smiling a dark smile. She crossed by Amy, who felt her pass like a cold breeze.

Nobody else seemed to see it, or sense it, but Amy suddenly did—something was not at all right, and it had something to do with the missing twins. Amy was suddenly sure, and looked around for Liz or Rat, but her friends had wandered off. Kelly must have picked up on what Amy was feeling, because she stopped and looked her straight in the eye, and for a split second her false smile flickered, then pulled back tight. "Welcome to Cyder Island," she said.

Her breath stank of onions. . . .

Amy was very glad to see Liz reappear. Amy started to whisper something about Kelly, but Liz grimaced. "I'm not ready for this; let's look around."

"Where's Rat?"

"Who knows?"

They wandered around. Most of the people there shared one thing in common: they had all been dragged to Cyder Island because of this family support/vacation thing, but now it didn't seem so bad. As Liz said, it was almost like camp.

Amy saw Travis then, gathered around a group of guys playing with the fire; whenever the breeze changed the smell of the flames blew across Amy. It smelled of summer. Liz nudged Amy as they walked, pointing guys out. They weren't who Amy noticed. "Oh, no."

"Oh, no, what?"

Nodding in the general direction, Amy said, "My sister Katie."

"Yeah?"

"Yeah." Katie was clustered around a group of loud, older types, passing around paper cups and soda cans on the other side of the fire. Amy said, "I thought she was supposed to be up at the school."

Liz shrugged. "I told you how that worked. You going to tell your mom?"

"No. But if I play this right I won't be loading the dishwasher for a while."

"A girl into blackmail. I like that."

"So, hello, and hey, there." It was Travis, with a ruffled brown-haired guy, standing close and speaking over the music. Having seen Amy and Liz, he hadn't waited for them to walk over; he grabbed his buddy and intercepted them. "So say hello to Dave."

"Amy and *Liz-a-beth*," said Travis, indicating he already knew Liz. "So how you doing?"

"Better than some, not as good as most," answered Liz. "I've already had one too many encounters with the twilight zone for one night . . ."

Liz told her Rudnick twins story. Grinning, Travis looked at Amy and said, "So at least I know who you've been hiding out with."

Rat came over then, grabbing Liz by the shoulder. "Melissa's over there," she said, very seriously. "She knows the Rudnick twins." Rat pulled Liz off with her and Dave didn't wait for an invitation; he followed.

Keeping half an eye on the group her sister was hanging with, Amy watched them go and then said to Travis, "I met your other buddy today, the pirate with the phony eye patch."

"Wally? Yeah? Isn't he great?"

"He's crazy."

"But not dangerous."

"Don't you think it's weird that he doesn't look that old?"

"What are you talking about? He looks old."

"Not if he really sank a boat sixty-four years ago. I've been thinking about that. He'd have to be close to eighty, and he doesn't look half that."

Travis shrugged. "He's all right. He's got lots of stories."

"Is that what you want out of life? Lots of stories?"

"Sure. What else? Let's walk around and find some."

They did; Travis knew almost as many people as Liz. A lot of them were the same people, actually, except the opinions changed. People Liz dismissed as "Loser, weasle, and brainiac," were now, "Cease— for Cecil. Hates his name but he knows karate— watch yourself." And, "Bruce, we'll stay away from Bruce—all the girls love Bruce, I'm too jealous." And, "Hey, this is Larry, total computer genius."

Different people, different perspectives, different worlds, thought Amy. She looked around for Liz, but couldn't see her. She couldn't see her sister, either. None of which mattered. She felt Travis take her hand and she let him; it felt good.

They got themselves a hamburger and some sodas and went over to sit on a log. Stacy Mohller, a girl who wanted to be an artist, sat on a big rock nearby with a sketch book. "Let me do you guys," she said.

Her mouth full and chewing, Amy shook her head but Travis grinned. "Great, do us with no clothes on."

"Hey!"

Travis laughed, pulling Amy over closer to him. Stacy frowned in mock concentration, her hand moving very fast with the pencil. Amy was sure there wouldn't be much of a likeness when she was finished, but she found herself surprised at the final result.

"Hey, that's me!"

"What did you expect?"

"I—"

Amy shut up—*something was happening*. The music suddenly started to switch off, one source, one tape deck at a time until there was a silent background. That killed the conversations; everybody seemed to drop into a confused hush, looking around, trying to figure out what was going on. Amy's first thought

50

was that somebody was in trouble over something, that something was going on. Maybe the party was being busted up by the adults from the house, or the cops even.

Amy heard some voices whisper: "The Caretaker, that's the Caretaker . . ."

Who?

Travis gestured over to where the crowd seemed to be looking to, up toward the pier where a shadowy figure was standing, looking down, and Amy almost jumped out of her skin; it could have been the Grim Reaper. Tall and thin, he wore a knee length grey trenchcoat and seemed emaciated, starving, pale skin stretched tight across his skull; it was as if he wore a chalky skin mask, but he wasn't grinning the skull of death or anything. He just *stared*.

Without looking to Travis, Amy now said to him in a voice drained of emotion, "Rule number one from the horror movies: Beware the mystery man . . ."

"No mystery," said Travis. "Wally told me about him. That's the Caretaker, the guy who watches over that shut-down fish cannery. He got hurt in the head years ago; he's not all there."

"No?"

"His brain I mean. They didn't fire him, though; not even when the owners closed up the place. Kept him on as the watcher."

"Watcher?"

"Eyes of the place. He never talks."

Amy stared up. "Wonderful. What's he want?"

"Just to look at us, I guess. Creepy."

"I heard he killed a little girl once," said Rat, reappearing at Amy's side without Liz or Dave. "Pulled her off into the bushes and killed her."

"A regular Hookman, eh?"

"Hookman?" Amy didn't understand what they meant.

Travis explained. "Hookman's the other story—you know, lover's lane killer and all that? But Caretaker, he's Cyder Island's biggest ghoul."

That made Amy's blood run a little cold. "Then why isn't he in jail?"

"Couldn't prove anything."

Amy looked at Rat and wondered if she was thinking the same thing: the Rudnick twins?

The Caretaker stood there above them, still staring. Maybe this was some weird game Liz, the horror movie star, liked to play on her new friends, but Amy felt herself shudder, another number one rule from the horror movies: don't look the bad guy in the eyes. She remembered the nightmare of dreaming someone was pressed up against her bedroom window, peering in. *What if it was somebody like that?*

5

After what she had seen looking down from the cannery pier, the moonlight off of the black water seemed to Amy, as they walked home, like nothing less than visible death, the shimmering of the light souls reaching out for heaven. *Or wherever*.

Gruesome thought; she shook it off, kept walking, but Amy was having a hard time not being nervous. Travis and Dave were ambling with them back up the beach. Rat pointed out that they were perfectly capable of getting home by themselves, but Amy—still nervous about the apparition of the Caretaker—was glad for the company. Besides, she was really getting to like Travis.

Dave, on the other hand, was much louder and more aggressive; probably just right for Liz. "You guys ever go rock diving?" he asked.

"What?" Liz didn't understand, and neither did Amy.

"Better than bungee jumping," explained Dave. "We've got about a seventy-foot sheer drop straight into a cove."

"I don't think so," said Liz.

"Come on, you'll love it. It's on the other side of the cannery."

This got Amy's attention. "What are you talking about?"

"The Caretaker's cannery, that's where we dive from. Very scary place. It's cursed."

"What do you mean, cursed?"

"Very high accident rate at the cannery, employees were dropping like flies, that's what Wally says. Says they probably killed more people than were finally laid off when the doors closed."

"Yeah?"

"The Caretaker's house of former dead fish," said Dave in his spookiest voice. "There's your new movie, Lizzie. They used to can salmon there, or tuna, or whatever. Now they manufacture cat food out of stray tourists."

"Beyond gross." Liz scrunched her face.

"So where do you dive from?" asked Amy.

"Off the factory side; it's seventy feet straight down."

"You could break your neck like that."

"Better than electrocuting yourself on a roof."

"I think you're a nut."

"I've been called worse," said Travis. "Problem is you can't even get there from the beach, not without going over all those rocks at the point. So you have to go through the factory grounds, and hope the Caretaker doesn't see you. Not that he'd be much bother, I guess; he never says anything to us."

"He looks like the Grim Reaper."

"You should see me in the morning," said Rat.

"Did you guys smell Kelly's breath?" asked Dave.

"I did," nodded Liz. *"Phew."*

"Smelled like dead onions," said Amy. "Same as Wally's."

"Halitosis," nodded Travis. "My Uncle John has it."

"I guess they don't sell enough toothbrushes on this island," said Rat. "Maybe we should all pitch in and buy her some mouthwash."

"Or Certs," said Liz.

The others all laughed and were talking about something else before Amy could make her point; besides, Dad always told her she could laugh about anything except another person's physical problems. Liz nudged her before she could change the subject back. "This is you, don't forget where you live."

Amy looked up at the bungalow; she hadn't recognized the house from the beach side. There were a couple of lights on, but it seemed very quiet. "Thanks. See you guys later."

Travis walked Amy up to the door. "Keeping yourself off the roof?"

"Yeah," said Amy. "But the TV's still all fuzzy."

"It doesn't really get much better," said Travis. "All the TV stations are back on the mainland. When there's a thunderstorm we don't have any TV at all."

"Yeah."

It was sort of an awkward moment, but Travis ended it by backing away. He did ask a question, though. "You doing anything tomorrow? Want to go bike riding?"

"Bike riding?"

"Yeah. We could go to the quiet beach on the other side of the island, go swimming, maybe?"

"Sure. Yeah. But you're not pushing me off of any rock cliffs. I'm not going anywhere near that dragon."

"Dragon?"

"That cannery. Looks like a big sleeping dragon to me."

Travis grinned. "No problem."

Amy nodded and Travis scooted himself back over to where Dave, Liz, and Rat waited, talking. Amy wondered if Liz actually liked Dave, or was just putting up with him for her sake. Why would she bother? Oh, well. At least she was making friends.

When she got back to the bedroom she pinned the picture of her and Travis on her bedroom wall. Stepping back to admire it, she noticed then that Sarah wasn't in her bunk; the bed was still neatly made, as if it had never been slept in.

She walked across the hall and knocked before going into Brian's room. The light was on, he was kicked back reading a stack of comic books and listening to the clock radio in the room. "Where'd you get the comics?"

"Some guy."

"What?"

"It's okay, Carlos knows him. He's got a zillion of them."

Amy frowned; something to maybe mention to Ma. "Where's Sarah?"

"What?"

"Where's Sarah?"

"I thought she was with you."

"What?"

"Isn't she with you?"

Now Amy was confused. "Why would she be?"

"Don't blab it." Brian kept his voice down, leaning closer. "I thought she followed after you."

"What?"

"She went after you. Snuck out, said she could watch the videos any time, she wanted to go to the beach party thing, too; didn't she catch up?"

"And you just let her?"

"I'm not her keeper."

"Brian, she's only seven."

"So? What was going to happen? She went with you."

What could happen? Well, for one thing she could have a seizure out where nobody could help her. Amy didn't say any of that, though. She said, "She didn't go with me. I didn't even see her."

It was Brian's turn to frown. He looked around for a minute, as if the answer was going to be there for him somewhere else in the room; it wasn't. "Do you think we should tell Ma?"

That would get Sarah in big trouble, probably—Amy suddenly realized—the worst trouble she had ever been in. Even though Amy was now mad at her younger sister, she was in no hurry to make her life miserable. Amy remembered all the times Katie got her into trouble over things, the way that made her feel betrayed. Then she remembered Katie at the party, and wondered if Sarah had wound up with her. That didn't seem likely. She asked Brian, "Did you look around outside?"

"Why should I?"

"Because it's almost ten o'clock and your little sister is outside somewhere. Get up off your butt."

Brian did, dropping his comic book on the bed. Their mother was back in her room, so Amy took him out the back door to help look around. The surf was chugging in and out, a pleasant melody, but for a very scary second Amy pictured her sister out there drowning.

Very scary. But Sarah wouldn't go out in the water, no way. She could barely swim and she knew it; she also knew what could happen if her epilepsy hit while she was out there away from help.

Amy closed her eyes. "I think we need to tell Ma."

"Yeah," agreed Brian. He confessed: "I'm getting a little scared."

"So am I."

Amy frowned. Time for a search party? Time to call the cops? Were there any cops to call? Who could you call?

Amy went to tell Ma what was going on. She took a deep breath, and then she just said it: "I can't find Sarah."

"What?"

"Sarah's gone," said Amy. "I just looked around and can't find her."

Her mother didn't even look up from her page. "You'll find her."

"What?"

"The summer's just starting."

Huh? "So what does that have to do with anything?"

"Well, I'm assuming this Sarah girl you want is on the island."

"This 'Sarah girl'?" Amy blinked back her confusion, taking a deep breath. "Ma, what are you talking about? Of course she's here."

"Then relax. It's a small place, you'll bump into each other eventually."

"Eventually? Ma . . ."

"What, Amy?"

"Aren't you going to help us look for her?"

"Look for who?"

"Who? Sarah."

Now Mrs. Meyer closed her book. "And why are we looking?"

"Because she's only seven years old."

Mrs. Meyer crinkled a frown. "Amy, what are you talking about?"

"My sister. Your daughter."

"Katie?"

"Not Katie, Sarah."

"Who?"

"Sarah."

"*Sarah?* Amy, again, *what* are you talking about?"

"I'm talking about your daughter, Sarah, my little sister."

Amy got a really sick feeling then, because all of a sudden Mrs. Meyer laughed, and that was startling and scary because Ma was laughing and saying, "Amy, I don't know what you're talking about. You don't have a little sister Sarah. Don't you think two daughters are more than I can handle as it is?"

6

The Rudnick twins; now Sarah. Amy caught on right away. Caught up in her laughing, Ma didn't understand what was going on, and she was sitting back in bed with a book across her lap making some kind of joke.

"Ma, please, listen."

"Please? Not *puh-lease*?"

"This is serious; Sarah could have had one of her seizures—"

"What?"

"Her epilepsy—"

"Epilepsy?"

"Ma, come on—"

"What is it? Amy, I can't understand what you're trying to talk about. Who do you know that has epilepsy?"

"Who? Sarah does."

"Sarah who?"

"Your daughter Sarah."

"My what? I don't have a daughter Sarah. This is getting less and less funny, Amy. I don't think jokes about—"

"What jokes? I'm not trying to be funny."

"Come on. I'm reasonably sure that if I had a daughter I'd remember her, don't you think? Pregnancy and childbirth are a couple of those things that stick with you, trust me."

"Well, an aggravating little sister sticks with you, too, trust me."

Ma didn't say anything to that; she shook her head and tried to change the subject. "How was the party?"

"What?"

"The beach party, did you guys enjoy it?"

Now Amy just stared at her mother, suddenly feeling as if there was some strange distance between them. "The beach party? Ma, aren't you going to get up?"

"No, Amy, I'm not getting up. I'm trying to enjoy my vacation. Why don't you go and try to enjoy yours?"

"Vacation?"

"Go on, Amy, just go on."

Absolutely insane. Amy went back across the hall to the room they were sharing to grab something of Sarah's, anything—a toy, a doll, her medicine— anything to shove in Ma's face and make the point. She couldn't find anything handy. She pulled open the dresser drawers and at the same time she realized this Amy felt her chest go tight, very tight, like an asthma attack; she couldn't breathe, couldn't even choke out a cry for help.

Sarah was gone. Not just her, but all her stuff.

Ripping through the room, Amy tossed the place but couldn't find anything. Not clothes, not toys, not even Sarah's empty suitcase. Someone had come in and taken all of her things.

A break in? That didn't make sense—all of Amy's stuff was exactly where she left it. The top two drawers of the dresser were full of her stuff, the bottom two—those closest to Sarah's reach so to prevent her from pulling the dresser over on top of herself—were empty. Easier for a little kid to get to, but not for a teenager or adult—why bend down to rob the kid's clothes and underwear? Especially when there were clothes and jewelry in the top two drawers? If someone had broken in, it wasn't by accident that they had only taken Sarah's belongings.

Which didn't make any sense. How could anyone have done it? How would it be possible? All of Sarah's stuff had been there earlier, the house had never been empty, and now it was gone.

Just like the Rudnick twins, and their mother acted like she didn't remember them either. *Oh my God. . . .*

Dad. Amy wrapped her arms around herself and squeezed. If Dad was here he could handle things, he could fix things, he'd take care of them. But Dad wasn't here.

"What are you doing?"

Brian was standing there in the doorway now, his hands in his pockets, waiting for Amy to tell him something, what to do, maybe. He was starting to look a little scared himself.

"What's going on?"

"I don't know."

"Mom's acting weird." He looked around, as if fearful of being overheard.

"I know."

"What about Sarah?"

"I don't know. Give me time to think."

"Amy . . ."

"Something's going on here. Give me some time to think."

Brian nodded, shutting up for a minute.

Again and again, Amy tried to think this all through,

but doing so without distraction was almost impossible. Could this be some weird game, a scam Liz and Rat were running on her? They seemed cool enough, but Liz was a horror movie queen, and who knew about movie people?

No. Sarah was missing and Ma would never be in on a joke like that. She wasn't just acting weird, she was acting creepy. Creepy because there was no avoiding the scariest thought—did Mom have something to do with Sarah's disappearance?

Oh my God. And there were the Rudnick twins. . . .

No, no way—that wasn't possible. Ma wasn't some sort of monster, she was just Ma. Just the same lady who had brought them all to the island.

Then Amy remembered—the pictures.

The stupid Polaroid photographs Ma took on the boat, they would prove everything. Except for what happened to the clothes and toys, maybe, but that could all wait.

She walked quickly back down the hall to her mother's room. "I need to see the pictures."

"The what?"

"The pictures, the pictures you took on the ferry."

"They're put away."

"Ma, *puh*-lease. I need to see it."

"What's this about?"

Swallowing, Amy said, "You know what it's about."

Ma shook her head and got up, going to her own dresser and pulling out the batch of pictures. Amy flipped through them once, twice, all the time getting more and more sick and desperate.

Sarah was in none of the pictures.

"This isn't possible."

"What isn't possible?"

Amy was looking at the posed photo, the one with her mussed hair, the family shot. She remembered Sarah standing right beside her while Ma snapped the picture, but Sarah wasn't in it. How could a person disappear from a photograph?

It wasn't possible.

Was it?

Amy dropped the pictures back on the bed and wandered back into the hallway, feeling sleepy and lost. She could hardly breathe, because the pictures were real, too real, and the questions were obvious. Was Sarah ever in the picture? Did Amy have a little sister? Or was she going crazy?

Dad. That was it, Amy realized it in an instant: she needed to call her father.

The phone booth stood in silhouette on the town common, the sole light flickering down from a light pole above. Amy got there after leaving the bungalow and heading up the road—not the beach—toward town. The idea of being on the beach with that Caretaker guy possibly still about made her very nervous. Being summer, the trees of the nearby park were still in bloom but nevertheless a few leaves blew about the booth's base. It was an old style English phone box, red with thick wide framed windows as opposed to big Plexiglas planes. The glowing sign up top said TELEPHONE.

Dad. If she could just get hold of Dad he could fix things, no matter what was happening. He was smart, he was strong—nothing scared Dad. He'd jump on an airplane, come out and *fix this*.

Amy dropped a quarter in the coinbox and dialed, trying to call her father collect back in Ohio. What was the time difference? No, its the same time there, she thought. The operator helped her with the call and allowed it to ring six times, but there was no answer. "Would you like to try again later?" asked the operator.

"I need to . . ."

"Yes?"

"I . . ."

Amy hung up the phone.

There was a plastic card next to the coinbox that read EMERGENCY SERVICES. Police, fire, medical, and coast guard. The coast guard mention was different from phone booths back home, but Amy thought it made sense since they were on an island.

Stuck in a horror movie, Amy thought then, very suddenly. All her life she had anticipated this sort of situation, expected it. Readied herself for it; she always figured you wound up in a horror movie sooner or later, because if nothing else everybody had their own private horrors: snakes, sharks, monsters, math class.

So this was her movie, and now it was her movie. The number one thing in any horror movie—the moment of decisive action by the hero. Amy called the police.

This time the phone rang three times. "P.P.D.," answered the man on the other end.

"Excuse me?"

"Patience Police Department? You calling Cyder Island?"

"I'm on Cyder Island."

"Then you've got the police."

"Excuse me?"

"Come on, what'cha need? There's a good movie on."

What kind of cop was this she was talking to?

He sounded like an obnoxious twerp. "I need some help."

"We can help you. Probably."

"Probably?" Amy groaned.

"Who am I talking to?"

"My name is Amy Meyer; I'm fifteen years old. I have a little sister named Sarah, she's seven. She's missing. And she's got epilepsy."

"Epilepsy? What's that?"

What's that? "Maybe she had a seizure, I don't know, she doesn't always take her medicine like she's supposed to; I know she's missing."

"Missing?"

"She's gone. Something's happened to her I think."

"Could I have your name again? No, wait a second. Let me turn the TV down . . ."

Amy repeated it, and gave the address of the beach bungalow as best she remembered it. "That's where we're staying. I'm not there right now, though."

"So where are you now?"

"In the phone box on the common. In town. I was looking for her, and I tried to call my dad, and then I called you guys."

"Is your father staying with you at the bungalow?"

"No, my mother."

"You said your name was Amy?"

"Twice, I said it."

"Well, *excuse me*. Okay, Amy. You stay right where you are, and I'll have someone come see you."

"And find my sister?"

"Whatever works, I say."

Click. Startled, Amy hung up the phone. What kind of a way was that for the police to act? She tried a collect call to her father again, but he still didn't answer. The temperature outside seemed to be dropping, and she shivered, standing there in the booth. None of this seemed real, but she knew that it was. Unless it was a very real, very scary dream.

So Amy waited, leaning back against the phone, and she made the mistake of closing her eyes for a moment.

Which was when she heard the snap, behind her, and she felt the sensation again—the same sick feeling she had lying in bed before, convinced some hideous face was pressed against the window of the bungalow, peering in. She was suffering the same sensation now; whatever made her feel that way was near again, and if she opened her eyes to see, something terrible could happen.

Or not. *Crazy. This was crazy.*

But she was in her own horror movie now, Amy was, and it felt real, more real than any of those silly step on a crack and break your mother's back games, more real than any of those race to the house door in the dark because there's a murderer chasing us games; this was lower lip trembling, keep your eyes closed tight scary.

One of those rare moments in life where madness reigns. A plunge from a high building or bridge, a lost grip, that terrible moment when balance shifts and the stomach realizes first—long before the brain—that the body is falling, falling—fate racing toward you without remorse, with no delay. Car wrecks are a lot like that, the last, sickening realization that collision is inevitable.

Amy felt exactly like that now. Stuck in that phone booth, her back flat against the phone, her eyes closed tight, she felt as if she was being chased, wanted, pursued across some terrifying plain. Her heart? It was pounding beyond belief.

Somebody was behind her, behind the phone booth. She was as sure of that as she was of her shuddering breath. And if she kept her eyes closed maybe it would go away.

And maybe it wouldn't.

Without opening her eyes Amy reached forward and pushed open the door, running now, racing and slipping; she felt her balance go a second before she crashed down on the ground, hurting her knee and opening her eyes at the same time that groping hands grabbed her, pulling her back fast before she could even start to fight.

"Hey!"

After realizing she wasn't dead, or dying, Amy didn't fight or strike out; she saw right away she didn't have to, even though her heart seemed to be pounding in her ears.

The person before her was a tall, thin woman with long restraining fingers and a beak for a nose. About Ma's age, her hair was stringy and short; she squinted in the light and wore a blue jacket and a badge. She carried a flashlight, but wore no gunbelt. "Did you call the police?"

"Yes." She still felt the panic sensation; whatever it was watching her was close, very close.

The policewoman cleared her throat; it sounded as if she was always in the process of clearing her throat. "Are you Amy?"

Nodding, Amy started to answer when the night was pierced by a scream; an absolutely inhuman, lost sound of prolonged agony which scratched at the soul. Amy felt sick, smaller. "What was that?"

The police woman looked around, listening, but unconcerned. "How should I know? Sounds like an animal out there somewhere."

"An animal?"

"Aaaaaaaaiiiiiiieeeeeeggggghhhh!"

It was a sound from hell, something being dragged toward eternal torment; it was a low sound, a last sound; in the silences between the victim was probably trembling, in mid-collapse. Amy felt that way now. "That can't be an animal."

"Sure. Probably a cat."

The scream came again, a long desperate sound which could have been a cat, might have been a cat, but only if the cat was suffering the pain of the ages.

"Aaaaaaaaaiiiiiiieeeeeeghhh!"

The policewoman giggled.

"Oh my God."

"Nothing, nothing, don't worry about it."

"What kind of a cop are you? That's a scream. There's kids out there."

"Nah, probably just a squirrel being killed by something." The cop laughed.

That statement and the laugh unnerved Amy. She didn't expect the policewoman to go off on a long chase to save a cat's life, but she also didn't expect what was obviously gruesome pain to be so easily dismissed.

The policewoman seemed to read the thought, saying, "Gotta get real, girl. Things die sometimes on the island. Don't they die back where you live?"

Get real? "That sound."

"Aiiiiiiiiieeeeeeegggggggghhhhhh!" Again.

Without meaning to, Amy found herself standing close to the policewoman, who quickly returned to business. "So your sister ran off?"

"Yes. And there's something else, maybe. I think."

"Okay. I've got the patrol car, let's take a drive around and look."

"Aiiiiiiiieeeeeegggggggghhhhhh!"

Amy jumped. All of a sudden being away from the common and inside of a safe car was where she wanted to be, because if this was a horror movie she had to remember the number one rule: anything could happen. The scream came again, and Amy shuddered; was Sarah out there somewhere listening to that?

Then came a worse thought: *What if that was Sarah?*

7

The horrible sound was harder to hear, easier to ignore inside the car, especially when the policewoman introduced herself as Chief Errett surprising Amy. "You're the police chief?"

They were in a police car, driving the winding road back toward the bungalow, and the policewoman nodded. "Sure, why not? I'm the fastest draw on the island. Want to see me shoot something? A target, I mean? Check this out." Reaching under the car seat she pulled out a large pistol and handed it to Amy. "What do you think of that, huh?"

The woman was crazy. Here we go. Something trembled; best to ignore it, except Amy realized it was her, and then she realized why. *The police chief's breath stank of onions. Sweet, oily smelling, rotting onions left too long beneath the kitchen cupboard.*

Amy swallowed. "So, you're an islander?"

"Yeah. So what?"

Oh my God.

What? *Why?* What did it mean? Did it mean anything? So these people had bad diets and bad breath, what was she freaking about? She was freaking about Sarah, that's why, and Ma, and the Rudnick twins—just ask Liz or Rat—and it didn't take a rocket scientist who'd sat through a few slasher movies to figure

71

out that she was in a lot of trouble if she started ignoring the weird feelings, the weird sounds, the weird smells.

"Why do you care if I'm an islander?" The woman looked suspicious, and her frowning question made Amy feel a little sick. She took back her gun from Amy. "Something wrong?"

The ax murderer goof; Amy grimaced because she was real close to making the ax murderer goof, and that was the number one thing in any horror movie— the guy walks into a room, sees the killer there with a bloody weapon and boldly says something incredibly stupid like, *"Hey, you're the ax murderer—I'm going for the police!"* when what he should have done was pretended to see nothing.

Amy tried to pretend like she saw nothing. "Huh? Well, I didn't know you were the police-chief person, I mean. On the phone I talked to this guy—"

Again the onion smell. Smells were tiny, microscopic particles of the original object, Amy knew, which meant that the stink was coming from inside of the woman's body and passing into hers. Another shudder. The policewoman said, "That was Tony. He works the graveyard; we don't get that many calls."

"You've only got two police officers?"

"We don't get many calls."

"So how long have you been chief?"

"Since 1963."

"1963?"

The policewoman hesitated, again clearing her throat. "I mean I've been on the force since then; I worked my way up."

Amy felt that smell and the chill again. "That's still thirty years. You don't look that old." *Nobody around here looked that old.*

72

Again the frown. "Let's worry about the call you made, all right? Why am I out here now? It's pretty late."

Remembering again the ax murderer goof, Amy explained again about Sarah, including how she might have had an epileptic episode and might be wandering around embarrassed, ashamed to come home. As Amy did this she hesitated, because if the police chief was part of some weird islander conspiracy or something, then why didn't she just kill her or something?

Why would they play around with her?

Chief Errett drove very slowly, using the spotlight of the police car to shine off the road—just playing with it a lot, it seemed, every once in a while she would move the light from the hedges and yards they passed to someone's window and laugh. "Was your sister at the beach party tonight with you?"

"No." Then Amy recalled the intrusion of the man they called the Caretaker, and that gave her a scary thought and she said it. "That Caretaker guy, he was so creepy. Maybe he got Sarah or something?"

"Caretaker? Nah, he's the nicest old man on the island."

"So maybe he's a pervert or something."

"You shouldn't accuse people like that."

The car rounded the next bend and Amy realized she was home; the policewoman had brought her straight home. "Aren't we going to keep looking?"

"We did look. We've been around the island once. What do you want to do, drive around all night? Let's go inside and talk to your mother."

"What about my sister?"

"Let's go inside and talk about that, too."

Feeling sick, but relieved to be back close to people she knew, Amy followed the policewoman up to the

73

bungalow door, which had opened at the sound of the police car rolling up.

Ma had the screen open and Amy went in, followed by the policewoman. Amy was directed to the couch, and Ma held up her hands in apologies to the police officer. "I'm so sorry about all of this. What Amy has done is inexcusable."

"Not to worry," said the policewoman, suddenly acting much more stern and mature than she had in the car. She sure wasn't playing with her gun anymore; she'd left it in the car and she looked back to Ma, who told her very emphatically and obviously not for the first time that she had no daughter named Sarah, that it was easy to check, and that for some reason her middle child had decided to make this strange appeal for attention.

Amy's mother didn't say too much after the policewoman left, although Amy tried to. "I was looking for Sarah, this whole place is starting to seem way too weird. That cop lady is crazy."

"Crazy?"

"Yeah, and she smelled just like—"

"What?"

"Onions. Ma, all these islanders smell like onions. Dead, sick onions."

"Amy . . ."

"It's not just that. There's Sarah."

"I don't—"

"Remember Sarah. Come on, they're doing something to your mind, Ma."

"My mind?"

"Mom, think about it. You've got four kids, think about it."

Her mother appeared to do so, folding her arms, but she said, "I count three, Amy."

"That's because they're doing something to you, to us. This is a bad place."

"Amy, I want you to look at me and answer this question very seriously. Do you understand me?"

Amy nodded.

"Were you drinking at that party?"

"No."

"What about drugs?"

"What? No way, I don't do that stuff."

"Did somebody give you something strange to eat, or drink."

"No, I'm fine. It's you guys. Ask Brian, he knows. He remembers."

"I did ask him."

"You did?" Amy felt her eyes go wide, her legs go a little bit wobbly.

"Three children, Amy. There's only three children."

"Three and Sarah."

"I'm not listening to this Amy. I think you should go to your room."

"But what about Sarah?"

"Now!"

Amy did, closing her bedroom door behind her and pacing a bit, trying to figure out what to do now, the empty bottom bunk laying into her that this wasn't over, although she was tired, so bone tired, and it would be so easy to climb up into bed, relax, drift to sleep, and forget. . . .

No!

The door opened behind her. She thought it was Ma, but it was Brian, sneaking into the room, looking confused. "What happened? Are you in trouble?"

"Trouble?"

"Why did the police come?"

"I wanted her to find Sarah."

"Who?"

That did it. Amy felt herself lose control, lose it totally and before she even realized her movement she had her brother by the shirt and was shoving him back against her bedroom wall. "Don't do this, why didn't you tell her? Don't tell me it's you too—"

"Amy . . ."

"You know Sarah."

His eyes wide, Brian said, "I don't know. Maybe."

"She's your sister."

"You and Katie—"

"Me and Katie and Sarah—"

"You're hurting me—"

"Why are you guys doing this—"

"Amy!" Ma was there now, barking.

The bark wasn't enough, not enough, anyway, because Amy didn't let her brother go, she couldn't. She was looking in his eyes, feeling herself trying to swim around in the blue of them, trying to see what he was seeing, feel what he was feeling, figure out what he was saying, why he was saying it.

Was he all right? Was he playing a game? Part of some game? Because if he wasn't, she was caught up in a bad one of her own. Was this a nervous breakdown? They talked about them all the time on TV. Was this what one was like?

"Amy. Let him go." Ma's hand was pulling Amy back by the shoulder, and she released her brother but glared at her mother, doing the best with what toughness she had left. "I'm calling Dad."

"So am I. Amy, you're scaring your brother and you're starting to frighten me."

"Why are you guys doing this?"

"We're not doing anything, Amy. And I can't figure out what you're doing. I think you should get to bed.

We've got a counselling session to go to tomorrow for Katie—all of us have to go. Maybe we do need it. I don't know why you're acting this way. Maybe we can figure it out."

Ma left, and even that was a question; this was like that body snatcher movie or something: *was that even Ma*? Ma would remember Sarah, a mother couldn't just forget about her own daughter, could she?

Except in your own private horror movie.

Amy felt herself going weak in the knees, and she slipped to the floor, her back against her bedroom door—her and Sarah's bedroom door—and she started to cry, for the first time in all of this, and she continued to cry, until she fell asleep there by the door. . . .

II

amy in wonderland

. . . . the killer had wept, too, but not then, much earlier, so much earlier on that summer night in 1959. Birdman, they had called him, birdman, birdman, smelly birdman. . . .

So he had tried to show them. And failed. The bloody shirt wrapped around the end of his arm, the throb that reminded him of the explosion, his missing hand, his muddled thinking, his failure. The killer had been screaming and bleeding so badly, wishing to die, crawling out into the sea to make himself die, make himself drown, and then. . . .

And then as he charged out into the stinging, salty surf, pushing himself past the strange bits of broken crate washing ashore as driftwood, the green-black hands of the Master had reached for him, taken him, and the killer could have been consumed, destroyed out there in the foaming waves, nine feet from the beach, but that wasn't what the Master wanted, that wasn't what the Master needed.

Save me.

The killer saw the Great Master's eyes then, the tight grip of the hands holding his head beneath the water, forcing his gaze. Half buried in the sand, beneath the low tide mark, the Master writhed in agony but was helpless to pull Himself out of the sea, on toward the beach because—although the killer didn't realize this then—the Master could not willingly cross unstilled waters. Before the challenge of the sea He was powerless.

Others knew this. Those who had trapped Him, immortal, they thought, in the homeland. Five hundred years before Napoleon stormed his armies across Europe they succeeded in humiliating Him, containing Him in the pine crate from which there could be no escape until they would pitch the crate overboard into the sea.

The Master had been betrayed by the children of his own disciples; the horror of that tasked him even in the torment of His personal damnation. The children! Their plan was to leave the Master forever on the floor of the ocean, a grave from which He could neither rise nor move.

And they very nearly succeeded, would have succeeded, save for the storm. That storm that seemed to rise straight from Poseidon's lair to take first their courage, next their ship, and finally their lives.

But that wouldn't be enough, couldn't be enough; because although the Master could not drown, He could suffer, and even as He was hopelessly trapped, the Master's every thought was on revenge. If He could not feast on those pitiful mortals who plotted the betrayal, then He would have it on children, all children.

The Master suffered, lost beneath the great sea, suffered tortures as none of His kind had ever known, but He knew as every immortal did that time—the enemy of all mortals—was His ally.

The Master's coffin was among those things set free by the disaster, and even as the broken ship settled to the ocean floor He remained inside the crate, caught in His private hell, as it moved—slow but sure through the process of erosion and current as well as the displacement of storms. Once in a turbulent month the casket shifted its position eleven miles; for two years it moved not at all. Storms and a sea quake during the time of the American Civil War brought it within sight of land, yet between the years when the Wright Brothers flew and a mortal launched something into space the casket made up hardly half the distance remaining.

Still, it did move, willed perhaps by the Master, absolutely by the world's magick which could be denied no more than electricity or gravity. And all the while, amidst the pain, the Master thought of revenge, revenge on the children, the children, all children.

Thoughts not so much different than those of the killer when he stumbled across the Master as He lay impossibly caught beneath the beach surf, trapped less than ten feet from freedom.

The moment when the killer fought to end his own tormented life.

Save me.

The killer trembled. How could he possibly deny the will of those eyes? His eyes? In this instant neither life nor death were so important as pulling the Master from the prison of the sea, up to somewhere where He could be safe, wield his power.

Save me, said the Master's eyes. Save me; I shall make you strong again.

Confused, lightheaded from the fear and loss of blood from his wound, wondering if these sensations and sights were real or illusions, the killer looked about as he pulled the Master's twisted, decaying

*corpse from the crashing water, searching for a place
to go, an avenue of escape, somewhere to drag himself
and the Master to where they might mend themselves,
rest for a while.*

Perhaps the old cannery. . . .

8

The family guidance counselor was a woman named Eunice Knoll; her office was on the Kensit School campus. Eunice Knoll wore her dark hair short, was dressed in an expensive looking purple blouse with lots of jewelry, and she was fat. Very fat. Her cheeks puffed in a cheery way, her legs bulged under her slacks, and the size of her fingers made them appear crammed together, as if there were too many digits on each hand.

Katie, Ma, and Brian sat in a circle of chairs rounded out by the round woman. Although she found it hard to sit still, Amy was with them and soon saw why the counselor was so fat. Inside the circle was a small table, and on the table a platter of treats which weren't just treats. Ms. Knoll explained. "I call this a snack session," she said.

Grinning, Brian said, "Wow. And to think I thought this all would be silly."

Amy gave her brother a hard look, because at first he remembered and now he was forgetting. What could be happening to his mind? Would it start happening to hers soon? What would become of Sarah then?

Dad. Amy had to keep telling herself this: Dad. Three times now she had tried to call him, and he wasn't home, but eventually he would be, Amy would explain to him what was going on and he would be out here in a flash to put an end to this madness.

Madness.

The counselor was agreeing with Brian. "This is a little silly," she said. "I use these sessions as sort of an icebreaker. Since bringing up certain subjects is often difficult, especially the first time, we'll talk about whatever it is that we're eating."

"Or what's eating us," said Katie.

"Ooh, very good." Ms. Knoll nodded. "Allow me to show you. These are the cupcakes of anger. If you're feeling angry and want to show it without talking about it, pick up a cupcake and nibble. There's lots of others. The chocolate frosties of betrayal. The licorice of lies. Carameled strawberries represent embarrassment. The whipped cream of evasion, evading the subject, and, over here the fudge of forgiveness. I have them all labeled in case you can't remember what you want to reach for. Let's all eat something, shall we?"

Amy leaned in close to the woman, sniffing at her breath. A little confused, Ms. Knoll asked, "Is something wrong?"

"Are you an islander?"

"What?"

"Are you one of these islanders? How long have you worked here?"

"Just since May. Why?"

"Amy . . ." Ma wasn't happy already.

"This is nuts," said Amy, sitting back. "Are you guys all crazy or what?"

"Amy . . ."

"Sarah is gone. She could be having a seizure, or be dead and nobody cares."

"Sarah?" Ms. Knoll didn't understand.

A little hesitant to explain, Ma said, "As I warned you, Amy's having a little problem of her own."

"Little problem."

"All of a sudden she's convinced we've lost a child, a sister."

"A sister with *epilepsy*," said Amy.

Ms. Knoll nodded. "Well, that's not so terrible. Not so unusual."

"Say what?"

"In a way she has lost a sister, albeit just for a while. Amy: you will get Katie back. You'll see."

"I don't care about Katie."

"Fine," said the oldest sister.

"You know what I mean, Katie, come on." Amy appealed to her. "Sarah. Tell them about Sarah."

"What are you talking about?"

"Come on."

"What about you, Brian?" They all looked to him now; he was eating from the snack plate, oblivious to any implied symbolism. Ms. Knoll asked, "Do you remember having a little sister Sarah?"

Brian thought a moment, then shrugged. "Maybe. I don't know."

"You don't know?"

"It is sort of weird. I do remember something. Something about that epilepsy. I remember something about *pheno*."

"Pheno?"

"Phenobarbitol," said Amy. "That's Sarah's medicine, he remembers that, he remembers her medicine."

"Which is a treatment for epilepsy," said Ms. Knoll.

"Which he only knows about because Amy told him and then banged him up against the bedroom wall,"

87

said Ma. "Please, don't get him started, too."

Ms. Knoll pressed the subject, though. "Did Amy tell you about this medicine?"

"Me and Amy talked about something. I remember that much."

"You remember speaking to Amy?"

"Yeah. Last night. She was real upset."

"Yes, I imagine that she was."

"I am not the crazy one," said Amy, standing now. "You guys are the crazy ones. Listen to you."

"The whole world is wrong and you're right?"

"That's happened before."

"Amy!"

"I'm not sitting around here. My Sissy could be dead."

Ms. Knoll waved Ma and Katie to sit down. "Let her go; Amy's upset. The new surroundings, the changes. This isn't as bad as it seems. This isn't as bad as it seems . . ."

Amy ran out of the room and out of the school building, but there wasn't much to run to on Cyder Island. She headed off back for the beach, back toward the bungalow, and she found herself calling out her sister's name, but there was no answer, never any answer, and she started crying, wondering now if maybe she wasn't losing her mind.

Maybe the world was right and she was wrong.

Maybe she was way beyond tired, beyond sick. Maybe she really was crazy.

So how did it feel to slip around the bend? To misplace one's marbles? To suddenly come up a few bricks shy of a load?

That would be better, being crazy would be for the best, because if she wasn't nuts, if she was still sane, then what was happening? What was going on?

She went to call Dad again, and—surprise, surprise—this time she got through. His answer was so sudden it shocked Amy into silence. "Hello?" he said. "Hello?"

"Daddy?"

"Daddy?"

"This is Amy."

"Amy, yeah, but since when do you call me Daddy? What's afoot? How's the vacation?"

"It was great but now all of a sudden I'm stuck in a horror movie."

"What?"

"It's a lot like a nightmare."

"Oh, yeah?"

"Something horrible is happening."

"What is? What are you talking about?"

Taking a deep breath, Amy blurted it out. "Do you remember Sarah?"

"What?"

"Sarah, Sissy, Sarah, do you remember—"

"Of course, I do. Sarah? What are you talking about? What's happened to Sarah?"

"You know Sarah?"

"Why wouldn't I know Sarah? Amy, what's wrong? What are you talking about?"

This island, the forgetting was only on this island! Amy wanted to yell for joy but there wasn't time; she had to explain, and she tried, telling Dad everything that had happened so far. The vanishing, the strange islanders, the way Ma and Katie totally forgot, Brian sort of forgot, and she remembered. The whole horror movie scheme of things.

"I told the police lady, and she didn't care because she's an islander, and I think these people are all

89

in on this together, whatever this is."

"And your mother acts like she doesn't remember Sarah either? You're sure of this?"

"Yes, if you don't believe me call her, talk to her."

"No. I'm coming Amy; I'll be there for you."

Again she wanted to cry. "Thank you."

"I'll have to catch a plane and rent a car. I'm not sure when I'll get there, but I will get there."

"When are you going to leave?"

"Now. Today. Just as soon as I get off the phone."

"Thank you for believing me."

"Why wouldn't I believe you, Amy?"

"I don't know. This is too weird. It's just so impossible for even me to believe."

"Just stay calm. No matter what else, I'm coming."

"Did you want me to call somebody? Tell someone else? The FBI maybe?"

"No. Don't talk to anyone; who knows what could be going on there? If it is like a horror movie you've got to remember the rules."

"I do."

"And rule number one is don't let on that you're on to them."

"I know."

"I want you to go back to the beach house and try to stay safe. Don't talk to anyone. I'm coming."

"Okay. Thanks, Daddy . . ."

Her father hung up, and so did Amy, walking away from the phone booth, away from the common, back toward the bungalow. Dad was coming, yes. He remembered Sarah, yes. Whatever horrible thing was happening to people's memories didn't affect the world, just the island. Dad would come and take them all away from here.

But what about Sarah?

And what if—*no, please no*—what if Dad lost his memory when he got to the island?

Not worth thinking about.

"Ahoy! Bright afternoon to you!"

Startled, Amy realized then she had wandered back in the direction of the wrecked house and beached *Tangerine 2*, and that wasn't good. Stubby fingered Wallace McFlint was there, stumbling around doing things as always, and this time Travis was there with him. Travis looked a little offended at the sight of Amy, and he carried on what he was doing, securing something to the deck.

"What brings you out and about today?"

Amy didn't even know what to say. Standing there, she just looked around. Old Wally was an islander, and they were probably all in on this together. Whatever it was.

Travis finally came down and said something. "I went by your house with my bike but nobody was there."

"What?" The statement made absolutely no sense to Amy, it was as if he was talking in a foreign language or something.

Travis jumped down from the deck and walked over. "Bike riding? Remember? We were supposed to go bike riding?"

"No."

"We were."

"What? No, maybe—that's not what I meant."

Now it was Travis's turn to look confused.

Trying not to be overheard by Wally, Amy tried to explain herself. "Something bad happened to my sister."

"Your sister? What? Your little sister?"

"You remember her?"

"Of course I remember her, you were trying to fix the TV for her. You almost fried yourself, why wouldn't I remember?"

"You'd be surprised."

"What's wrong?"

Amy explained, thankful for another potential ally; she felt much the same relief she had with Dad when he told her he was coming. "I didn't know if you were one of them, part of it."

"Part of what?"

"Whatever it is that's going on."

Travis turned, calling, "Hey, Wally."

"Not *him*," said Amy. "You can't tell him."

"Wally's all right, you can tell him anything."

The fisherman started walking over, but Amy said, "He's an islander."

"Yeah."

"And they're part of it. The vanishings."

"Vanishings?"

"What are you shouting about?" asked Wally, ambling over.

"Amy says her little sister has disappeared."

That startled Wally, and he looked around, as if fearful of being overheard. "When did this happen?"

"Last night."

"So soon?"

"What do you mean, so soon?"

Wally shook his head, turning and starting back up the beach.

"Wait a minute, you can't just say something scary like that. Tell us what you know, what's going on."

"There's nothing. You all go on home."

Travis was surprised by Wally's sudden change of

attitude. "But what about that sailing stuff you were going to show me?"

"I changed my mind. You children go along and leave me alone. Leave an old man alone."

Travis looked a little stricken, but Amy followed after him and said, "No way. If you know something about my sister, you tell me."

"There's nothing for me to tell."

"You know something. I can smell you people, you islanders, you know something, tell me." *So much for the ax murderer goof.*

"I'll tell you this much. You both stay superstitious, and get yourself some water between you and Cyder Island just as quick as you can. Before the full moon rises. I didn't expect anything to start so soon."

"What?"

Nervous now, "That's all I can say, I've done said too much."

Amy wondered: if a person could just leave, and Wally here wasn't part of it, why wouldn't he leave? She asked the question aloud.

He answered by saying, "It's not safe. Not safe to talk, nor safe to think. I can't talk about this; I'm no better than anyone else. You go away now. Get out of here before the full moon rises. Don't either of you two children come near my boat again . . ."

The killer became the Hookman in the depths of the cannery, long before any surgeon tried to help him. His hand replaced with the primitive prosthetic far from any daylight, although the Master did not cringe from the sun; that was a myth. Nor did He sleep all day; He never slept, He was, like all of His kind, cursed with insomnia. He didn't drink blood.

He was just undead. A vampyre.

The Master was a creature of myth, but as the Hookman was taught to kill with his new appendage he was pleased to discover most of the lore surrounding the Master was baseless, and the few with merit had wandered far afield from the truth.

It was one thing to call the Master a vampyre, quite another to truly understand vampyre nature, what such a creature was, how they managed to survive in a world of men determined to exterminate all of the Others. Since the beginning of time vampyres were part of earth's ecology, cleansing humanity's wake as bottom-feeding fish cleaned a river. The world took care of itself, and magick was as essential as gravity or electricity. The Master was not Dracula, He didn't thirst for young maidens and leave a trail of incriminating corpses; He thirsted for life and left nothing. Not even the memory of victims which might betray him.

Except for the children, those blasted children with their curious, hungry minds so hard to fool. As the Hookman came to serve the Master, spending many pleasant hours listening to his lectures he also came to understand this problem; all of life is so much more real, so much more vivid to children. The Hookman remembered his own experiences; summer fireworks, the Halloweens, the Christmas mornings, all bright and—even as an adult—impossible to forget. But for a child, before the fading began, every day was like this.

The Hookman and the Great Master discussed this often; as He regained strength a certain professorial side arose in His personality. After all, He was an immortal creature whose favorite subject had become the study of His own existence. Why wouldn't—why shouldn't—He pass along some of what He'd learned?

Children? Oh, you could fool them, eventually; some more easily than others. Distractions helped. It was a difficult task, though, and impossibly dangerous. After all, it had been the children who had caught on in the Old Country; they would always be the most dangerous element in any new land. So when He finally came ashore in America, pulled onto this island in the arms of the Hookman, the Master's first object had been the elimination of all the island's children. He used them as a source of strength, taking all of their energy and excitement and bright intelligence and, most importantly, making them go away.

This act, this taking, was called the sending; a much more pleasant term than something cruel, like the eating. When the Master did a sending, or when He chose to allow one of the Others to send for someone, that someone simply disappeared. Even the Hookman didn't understand how the magick worked, all he knew

95

was it did work, and it was as terrifying a fury as the wrath of any god. To be sent for meant your vanishing, and with the exception of what few children might be aware enough to remember, the world adjusted itself around this new hole in its existence. The writer George Orwell long suspected people could be unmade; he was right.

They could be sent for.

Like the piper of Hamlin's legend, the Master did the sendings and He made the children go away, and the Hookman helped Him.

The Master was not Dracula, and the Hookman was not Renfield; but they were close. So very close. The relationship between them was different than the others, different because of what the Hookman was, what he had to be. The Master's new disciples— the islanders He reached for and touched and made into vampyres—they could be changed into immortal servants and slaves, chosen to surround and protect Him, nourished as necessary, but their powers were limited. Aside from the obvious effort to create no creature strong enough to challenge Him (any so inclined could just as easily be taken, sent away as easily as any child) the others by their very nature could never leave the island, never cross the water. The Hookman was different, he could be so dispatched, when needed; an emissary to the real world.

So the Hookman remained human, mortal, loyal to the Master, assured his ultimate reward was certain if he would wear his mask, join the world and somehow pretend to be what he could never be; serve without question, doing whatever cruel deeds needed doing, no matter how merciless.

The Hookman did this with a silent enthusiasm which startled even the islander vampyres; they were immortal creatures now, driven, yes, but even they had lapses, hesitations, fears. Definitely they retained their sense of humor. Not the Hookman, though; one thing was clear—forced to face either the Hookman or the Master, most of the chosen would have rather confronted the creature who changed them from human into hideous, onion-smelling undead monsters. Because the Master was not Dracula. But it was all too possible that the Hookman was the devil. . . .

9

Attemping to follow her father's instructions—as well as keep Ma calm (there was no logic in fighting against people who wouldn't believe you, anyway; more horror movie rules)—Amy allowed Travis to walk her home. She could not convince him to stay, though; not without saying more than she wanted. "I'm gonna go see what's going on," he said.

"I wouldn't if I were you," said Amy, wondering if perhaps she should lay on Travis her horror movie theory about life, especially life on this island. Probably not the best idea she had all day.

Travis didn't seem the type to take that sort of advice, anyway. "I'll be all right."

"That's what they all say. Just ask Liz."

"Right," said Travis, and as he left Amy found herself writing him off. There he goes, down the road, the big hero guy in every horror movie who grabs a flashlight and takes off to chase the chainsaw murderer. In the movies people were sometimes so foolish you didn't even feel sorry for them when they were violently done in.

Amy had no intention of being violently done in; she was staying home. So that's where she was when Ma returned later in the afternoon and the next terrible thing happened. Amy took the new development as calmly as she could, reminding herself all the while that if she was living a horror movie her fate was still in her hands, and possibly a lot of other fates as well.

Ma left again a few moments later, yelling something about running some things back up to Katie at the school; Amy didn't bother to reply. A short while later the pounding on the front screen door started.

The pounding that seemed to echo the pounding inside her head.

Braced to ignore this, ignore everything, Amy sat on the floor of her room, her back against the door, eyes on the sheet covering the window. Every once in a while she closed them, thinking reassuring thoughts: Dad was coming, Dad was coming, yes, but in the meanwhile Amy was doing her best to figure out how much danger she was in.

Most likely answer: *mega*.

Best definition of *mega*: a lot.

The pounding on the front screen wouldn't let up and she crept into the living room, only to discover it was Liz and Rat. Amy ventured to the door. It was hot outside, but there was a nice breeze coming in off of the ocean. "Hey," she said, very casual, deliberately calm.

Revealing nothing.

Rat was quiet, Liz slightly out of breath and she said, "Amy, I think maybe I'm going crazy. Normally that sort of thing doesn't bother me, but Rat thinks I'm going crazy, too."

"Get in here."

"Okay."

Amy brought them in, sat Liz down on the couch, playing the friendly ear, while Rat paced around the room. "You remember the Rudnick twins, right?"

That was an insult. "Of course I do."

"Let me tell you what I mean," said Liz. "It's crazy. You remember how we went over and their mom acted like she never even heard of them?"

"I was there."

"So was *I*, that's the thing. Rat was all into that, but I sort of let it slip. I don't know why, it just did, you know?"

"Slip?"

"And that makes you crazy?"

"No, *listen*." Liz tried to explain. "I remember the thing about the Rudnick twins being gone now, but nothing about *them*. Not even their faces. It's all starting to go away, everything about them in my head. Like an old photograph fading."

"Fading?" Slightly chilled, Amy turned to Rat, who said, "It's all still crystal clear to me. I remember them; I'd swear I always will. But I think the memory fades, if you're not careful. If you don't fight to remember."

Liz was shaking her head. "I swear, this is just like in one of my movies or something."

"Yeah."

"Definitely not good." Rat walked around some.

I remember Michael, I remember Michael. The singsong the homeless woman was doing downtown came to Amy at the same time as the way Brian went from remembering Sarah to hardly remembering her to not remembering her at all. *Oh my God—you did have to fight to remember! That's why Brian forgot, that's why Liz was forgetting, that's why the old homeless woman remembered her lost somebody. She was fighting to remember who he was, singsonging his name to herself!*

"See, here's the deal," said Liz. "I know that all happened—I mean I think I know—only now I'm

100

not as sure as I was yesterday. I keep thinking maybe it's just something I read about, or you guys told me about, or something I dreamed about."

"Okay," said Amy. "So you dreamed it."

"No," said Rat. "Because we just went by Stacy's house—the girl who drew your picture the other night? She's not there, and her brother Carlos was freaking out; says his dad and mom just went into the village like there never was any Stacy."

"Just like the Rudnick twins," said Liz. "Only I don't know if I remember that or not. It did happen, didn't it?"

"Yeah," Rat was serious, speaking to Amy. "It did happen, didn't it?"

Feeling a deep coolness inside, as if she had just spent hours mowing the lawn in the heat and then suddenly downed a long, tall glass of lemonade, Amy said only, "Let me smell your breath."

"What?"

Stepping close, Amy said, "Breathe." Liz did and next Amy went over to Rat, who frowned but then blew out some air on her. Satisfied, Amy sat down beside Liz and said, "I think maybe we're all nuts."

"Why?"

"My sister's gone, just like the others." Amy announced this very calmly, without emotion. *Shock? Was she in shock? When was Dad coming?* She told them what had been happening to her. "Just like everybody else who's disappeared, nothing special," she said. "Ma doesn't remember her, either."

"And you called the cops?" asked Rat.

"Yeah, they don't care. The cops are islanders, they're part of this, whatever it is. Haven't you noticed?"

"I don't know," said Liz. "Maybe. Everybody seems cool enough."

"Too cool. This is like that Paradise Island in the Pinocchio story, where they turn all the kids into donkeys? Only I don't think we turn into donkeys here. I think we just go away forever."

"That's . . ." Liz let her voice trail off.

Rat finished for her. "Crazy. It is crazy."

"Yeah? Brian's gone, too, now. Just a while ago, I guess. Ma came home without him and I didn't even ask. When Sarah disappeared I lost my mind and screamed and ran around. Now Brian's gone, too, and I just want to climb in bed and sleep."

"Sleep?"

"Ma came home without him and I'm supposed to believe he never even existed."

"Did you ask?"

Amy shook her head. "I'm through asking."

"Maybe she just let him stay in town or something?"

Amy stared at Liz, saying nothing.

"Sheesh . . ." Liz got up and paced around the room. "How could we all be crazy?"

"Maybe we've done it to each other," suggested Rat. "People make each other crazy all the time."

"We haven't known each other that long."

"Maybe not. Maybe it's the island."

"That I could believe. This place is crazy enough for a whole lot of people."

They all thought about it a long moment. "You know what's funny?" said Liz. "This is so weird I don't even feel scared; I just feel weird."

Amy considered this, but the terrible things were still happening—just happened again—and the best thing she had to hang on to was that Dad was flying to the rescue, and what he told her to do was hide, talk to no one. Which was fine; she didn't feel so much like being brave.

So what would happen if she stopped being so keyed up about all of this? Amy thought it, then asked it out loud. "I wonder if that's what happens when you just relax and let it wash past you, maybe you forget."

"I wasn't relaxed," said Liz.

Rat disagreed. "You're always relaxed. Even in the movies, that's why you played those parts. The girl who stayed calm while giant leeches ate her friends. I'll bet part of your mind can deal with anything, and that's why it's letting you forget so easy."

"Yeah," said Amy. "There's supposed to be a chemical in your brain that gets released when you're in a lot of pain. Keeps you from hurting too much. Maybe this is something like that."

Rat nodded. "Either that or we're in some kind of super shock."

Amy considered this. Maybe she *was* in shock. Shock, that could be. What were you supposed to do when you were in shock? Go to bed, sleep it off, try and dream and forget or . . . fight it?

Fight it, maybe?

No way. That's what every horror movie wants you to do. If you don't go fight the bad thing then there's no plot, just a slaughter. And who wants to watch a slaughter?

Rat and Liz were trying to think it through, though, which was exactly the wrong thing to do. "We remember," Liz was saying, thinking outloud. "I remember your brother and sister—you remember the twins."

"So?" Amy shook her head. "We don't count. We're not the people in charge, the police, the parents."

"But why would we remember if they don't?" asked Rat. "They couldn't all be in on something like this together? Could they?"

Amy shrugged. "Maybe our minds are tougher than we think, maybe it's harder for us to forget. Or maybe it just takes longer."

It was Liz's turn to hold the silence before speaking. "So we could just disappear, too?"

"I think probably we will."

They walked to the back of the house, Liz and Rat following Amy; all of Brian's things were gone, as if by magic. Impossible; they had been there when Amy got back, sent herself to her room, and now they were gone like a foggy mist when the sun rose.

Not a horror movie, thought Amy. Even in horror movies things had to make sense; all of Liz's movies made perfect sense. Everything wrapped up very nicely. This was more like *Alice in Wonderland*. She was seeing impossible thing after impossible thing, and starting to get used to it. After all, how many times could the mind be numbed? By now she could bump into a talking caterpillar and it wouldn't faze her a bit.

She looked in her own room. Oh, of course. The picture was gone from her wall, the one Stacy had drawn of her and Travis. What did that mean? That Travis was gone now? Or was it because of Stacy? After all, if she never existed she couldn't very well have drawn the picture. Or maybe Ma just pulled it off the wall because she didn't like it hanging there. All of a sudden Amy didn't just feel depressed, she felt ill. *This does not compute. . . .*

"We need to do something," said Rat.

"I did do something. My dad is coming to rescue me. Stay close and he'll rescue you, too."

"At this rate we won't be here when he makes it," said Liz. "We do need to do something."

"Hold it," said Amy. "Back off you guys, no way. Think about what you're saying. Pretend for a minute this is a horror movie."

Liz shook her head. "Yeah, but Amy I've been thinking about that creepy Caretaker guy, remember? I've been thinking—"

"No, hold it, forget it, wait a minute." It was Amy's turn to pace around, try and make her point. "I want you guys to think about horror movies."

"What?"

"Horror movies, the movies you've been in, Liz. As weird and scary as this is, just pretend it's another horror movie, okay? And this time we're all characters, a bunch of teenage girls stuck in a really terrible place where weird and terrible things are happening."

"Yeah . . ."

Rat thought about it, coming up with the next. "So if this is a movie, what happens next? What do those girls do then?"

"I'll tell you," said Amy. "They usually do something stupid like chase out after the monster; they go looking for the killer and they get knocked off one by one. Every movie is like that, so no way. We're not going anywhere, we're not doing anything."

"What?"

Amy had made up her mind, and she sat back on her bed, explaining herself. "I'll tell you what we're going to do. You're both going to call your moms and tell them you're spending the night with me, and we're going to lock ourselves in my room and do nothing but hide."

"Hide? That doesn't seem right. What about your brother and sister, what about the twins? Stacy?"

"What about them? If something happens to us, who's even going to remember them? Who's going to remember us?"

Liz hadn't thought of that. "Oh, my God . . ."

"We're making this home fort," said Amy. "And we're not leaving home fort until my dad walks in that door to help us. I don't care if the world ends . . ."

10

Liz refused to spend the night without a bag of her stuff, and Rat agreed, so against her better judgement Amy was forced to tag along as they went together to both houses, Liz saying on the way, "I don't know what's safer about your place over ours."

"I don't either," said Amy. "So what do you want to do? Do you want to forget it?"

"No."

"That's just her movie star pout," explained Rat as Liz gathered a T-shirt to sleep in, a change of clothes, a few other necessary things. "By this point in the plot she would be barking instructions."

Amy sighed. "I told you guys my dad's coming. If I'm not home he might freak or something."

Still unimpressed, Liz pressed, saying, "So what's your dad going to do? I mean, what's the point?"

"He believes us. He believes me."

"Does he? Maybe he'll forget once he gets to the island. Or maybe he's just saying that to keep you calm until they can get here to throw you in the laughing academy."

Amy didn't say anything; what could she say? She'd had the very same worry herself, but figured there was no point in sweating it. If Dad believed her, there was going to be hell for these bad guys to pay; Dad could be a tough guy when he wanted to be. These islanders might be spooky goofy monsters, but nobody who played video games and acted like a bunch of demonic juvenile delinquents was going to be able to take him on.

And if he didn't believe her. . . .

"Can we go now?"

"What are you worried about? It's broad daylight, I need to grab something in town. Don't you like it downtown? I do. It's just like a mall, isn't it great?"

"Yeah," said Amy. "It's great, it'd be a great town if I wasn't so sure the place has sold its soul to the devil somewhere along the line."

"Sold its soul. I'm so sure."

Half-tempted to abandon them and just go back home, Amy found herself tagging along with Rat and Liz when they went into town to do their bit of shopping. Rat still seemed almost as paranoid as Amy, but Liz was definitely clicking back and forth between carefree and casual. They hit the record store, the pharmacy, and the T-shirt shack; Liz taking her time in each. "Want to rent a video?" she asked next.

"No." Amy started walking back out of town, toward the beach house, and Rat was following, so Liz did the same, except Amy's attention was diverted by a sudden thought and she hesitated in front of one of the stores— the *Olde Bookshoppe*, it was called—saying, "Wait a minute."

Liz's tone was a little mocking. "I thought we were leaving."

"I want to run in here."

"So wonderful, a bookstore."

"She doesn't read," explained Rat.

Amy said, "So long as we're here I want to check something out."

"Check away," said Liz.

They went inside. "Good afternoon to you all," said the tall man behind the counter; Vern, the proprietor. "Can I help you find something?"

Amy shook her head. "We need to look around."

"Need to, or want to?"

"Want to, I mean."

"Browse away."

They did; Rat tugged on Amy's sleeve and she in turn pulled on Liz's; the aisles were cramped, there were way too many books, Amy thought as they ambled down the aisles. What happened if one of these heavy shelves crashed down on a person? Would it crush him to death? *Another wonderful thought.*

The section she was looking for was labeled OCCULT.

"So what is this?" asked Liz, glancing at the titles. "Devil worship and stuff like that?"

"I guess."

"I don't really want to get into that stuff. I've made movies with that stuff in it. Nothing good ever comes of it."

"So who does? What choice do we have?"

"So what do you think?" Rat asked Amy, as if the realization had just occurred to her. "Are you thinking about witches and warlocks and all that stuff?"

"I don't know."

They looked at the books; the titles were spooky. *His Satanic Majesty And Friends*; *Witchcraft and Sorcery In History*; *The Devil's Advantage*; *Demonology and The Study of Legion*; *Bloodsports of the Middle Ages*; *The Witches of Salem and America's Northeast*; *Secrets of the Undead.*

"There's an awful lot of them."

"What?"

"For this small island bookstore there's an awful lot of this creepy stuff, isn't there?"

"I wouldn't know. How much is enough?"

"Finding everything all right?"

That made them all jump; Vern laughed, having crept up on them from the other end of the aisle. "Looking for anything in particular? Ghost stories for the camp fire, that kind of thing?"

"Uh, yeah."

"Let's see what we can find for you." Vern ran his finger along the bottom of a shelf and Amy caught a whiff of sickly smelling onion in the air. No surprise.

"There's a lot of spooky stuff here," said the bookstore owner. "Werewolves, vampyres, ghosts, and goblins."

"What about disappearing people?"

Rat's question was blunt; Amy gave her a sharp elbow, but too late. Vern frowned, saying, "What's that now?"

Liz came right out and asked about it. "We were wondering if there's been anything written about people disappearing as if they were never born."

"Disappearing? You mean vanishings?"

"Yeah, right into thin air."

"Well, I don't know how thin the air is . . ." Vern shook his head. "Sounds like you've been listening to Old Lenore a little too much."

"Who?"

"Lenore. The bag lady. Isn't that where you heard that story?"

Amy remembered, suddenly chilled. *Michael, Michael, I remember Michael. . . .*

"Island's only homeless person," said Vern. "She really shouldn't even be still around here. She should

110

be in a hospital somewhere. Guess there ain't much government money for that stuff anymore."

"Why?"

Vern shrugged. "That old woman's still chasing after her own ghost."

"Ghost?"

"An imaginary friend. That guy she's looking for was never even born. She says somebody tried to kill her and her boyfriend on Smoke Hill way back when, but I doubt that crazy old woman has ever had a boyfriend."

Again Amy remembered the singsong tune, only this time she whispered it aloud, feeling haunted herself, as if the ghost was on her shoulder: *"Michael, Michael, I remember Michael . . ."*

They all looked at each other. Amy asked, "Could we just look around some?"

"Sure, I guess." Vern hesitated, but none of the girls made any move to look at anything, and finally he got the hint and moved off down the aisle. "Whatever works . . ."

They sorted through the volumes on the shelf: *Black Magick*; *Evil Curses You Can Learn*; *The Beginner's Book of Spell Casting*; *Vampyres*.

"Vampyres?"

"Seems simple enough," said Rat. "I thought the word was spelled Vamp-i-r-e."

"Vampyres?" Amy frowned. "What do you think it is?"

"Take a look." Rat and Amy flipped through the text together; it was a heavy black volume and inside there were several full color plates; illustrations of terrible things from the middle ages. Prince Vlad Tepes, *Vlad the Impaler* said the overly graphic plate caption.

111

"Yuck," said Liz.

"Scary stuff."

"*Sick* scary stuff."

The book contained hundreds of different vampyre myths, and they flipped through. "I always thought vampyres were vampyres," said Rat.

"I guess not. I guess there's different kinds."

Vampyres. They flipped through. Reading the legends, they came across many very scary alternatives to the Halloween/Dracula traditions, different ways to deal and fight with them. According to the book religious artifacts didn't always work, and some vampyres could get along just fine in sunlight—they might seem lethargic and tired, but they wouldn't die.

A few familiar methods were offered. All vampyres could be destroyed by a stake through the heart, or by fire. They were repelled by garlic, and most of all by mirrors.

"Why mirrors?" asked Liz. "Are they that ugly?"

"Sort of, yeah," said Rat. "Apparently the one thing most repulsive, most horrifying to the vampyre was the truth of his own nature, the reality of the horror he is. The thing a vampyre most fears is itself."

A few pages later they came across a particularly disturbing myth—one which told of a creature that ate souls, making it as if that person had never been born. "Hold it," said Rat. She sat down on the floor, crossed her legs and continued reading. Amy knelt down and read over her shoulder; the chapter was called *The Cleansing of Europe.* Part of it read:

Possibly the most misunderstood superstitions arising from the Middle Ages concern the witch and vampire purges which took place in the wake of the Children's Crusade to liberate Jerusalem from the "Heretics" who lived there. One hundred thousand children between the ages of five and seventeen left from their homelands following the example of the many noblemen and knights who had joined in the various crusades. Nearly an entire generation of Europe's children disappeared, however history notes that as they marched to the sea, their leaders claimed to have discovered and destroyed creatures of evil and supernatural pursuit, some of which they bore with them for final disposition in the sea. . . .

"I don't understand all of this," said Amy.

"I don't understand *any* of it," said Liz.

"What's this children's crusade? I've never heard of it. A hundred thousand kids?"

"We need to read this," said Amy.

Rat agreed, and they decided to buy the book except they didn't have enough money. They went through their bags, and came up short. "Come on, boss, pitch in," Rat said to Liz.

"Why can't we just read it here?"

"Come on, this is important."

Not very happy, Liz fished out a ten-dollar bill to add to the fund. On their way out, nearly at dusk, Liz said, "Hey, look, there goes Creepy."

"What?"

Amy looked up and saw the Caretaker, walking the street. Without even thinking she backed up, back into the doorway, hiding. Rat pulled Liz back with them.

"What's wrong?"

"Shut up."

They all did, watching. Caretaker walked in slow, unhurried steps, occasionally brushing at his face; his skull-face and black eyes made Amy shudder, worried he might see them. He passed by a mirror in a store window, turning quickly away. He started walking just a little bit faster.

What was he afraid of? Casting no reflection?

Amy grabbed the other two girls and hurried home.

11

As slumber parties go, theirs was more like a nervous cross between *Truth or Dare* and the *Twilight Zone*. Amy couldn't figure out whether they should be huddling in terror or just staying on their guard against whatever might be out there. After they got back to the house Amy, Liz, and Rat stayed in Amy's room most of the time, even after Ma got back and insisted on making them dinner.

"Don't you think it's weird?" Amy asked when they settled at the table. She was trying to get some reaction from Ma. The reaction she got was from Rat and Liz: apprehensive stares.

"What now?" asked Ma.

"Well, all the groceries you bought. If it's just you and me eating, I mean why did you buy so much . . ."

Frowning, Ma said, "Don't start, Amy; you know your father is coming in a few weeks."

Sooner than you think, thought Amy.

"Besides, groceries never go to waste. We can always have friends over. Like now."

"Usually at slumber parties we have pizza," said Liz.

"This isn't a slumber party," said Amy.

"Oh?" said Ma. "Then what is it?"

"Nothing," said Amy. "They're just staying over. To talk."

"Before it was beach parties, now just talking. Maybe I should be concerned. Well, I am sorry that this isn't pizza."

"It's okay, I'm not very hungry," said Rat.

"Neither am I," said Amy; her stomach was a little too queasy for that. Plates of messy brown noodles were passed around. Amy sniffed and hesitated. "Another failed experiment?"

"Beef stroganoff," said Ma. "Eat."

"Consume," agreed Liz, chowing down.

Amy spooned a lump onto her plate and listened as Ma asked Liz the same movie questions she had asked herself the first day. Only now they seemed even sillier, considering the situation. Unlike her and Rat, Liz's appetite seemed unaffected and she enjoyed talking about herself more than she'd admitted, and she got into it pretty well. Ma was happy. "It's nice to have something interesting to talk about," she said. "Dinner table conversation just isn't the same since Amy finished bringing home gory stories from her biology class."

"Eeew," grimaced Liz. "I don't want to hear about it."

"I should think your movies were worse than that."

"Yeah, but that was never blood. Just a lot of food coloring and clear syrup; looks really gross but it's not like cutting up a real frog. I just want to forget about all of that."

Rat gave Amy a knowing look.

"I think I need to go brush my brain," she said, going off from the table toward the bathroom. Amy actually watched the door, nervous that the big black-haired girl might never reappear, except she did.

"She's forgetting," Rat whispered.

"What?"

"Listen to her, it's all going away. Listen to her."

Amy did. Liz was very nearly totally back in the real world, she and Ma; it was as if the weird stuff didn't affect either of them at all.

After dinner they hunkered back in Amy's room and camped out. If it was a real slumber party they might have played games or intentionally tried to scare each other, but this didn't seem the right situation for that, since they were mostly flipping through the vampyre book, although Liz said, "This reminds me of that slumber party scene in *Gruesome Leeches II* where I pretended to have that monster burst out of my stomach; totally gross. Everybody was scared then, too."

"Yeah," said Amy, staring in horrid fascination at something on one of the pages. Then: "Wait a second, there was no slumber party in *Gruesome Leeches II*."

"Nah, we filmed one but then they went with the beach party instead. Left the slumber party stuff on the cutting room floor; Uncle LeRoy wanted somebody to get attacked right away."

"Besides, you're not scared anyway." This was from Rat.

"What do you mean?"

"You don't seem scared."

Liz shrugged. "I'm okay. I'm not looking at that horrible book like you guys are."

"I know," said Rat, quiet for a moment before she said, "So tell us, we need to know."

"What?"

Changed into a long *Beach Blanket Bozo* T-shirt, Rat stood up and looked very serious, saying, "Lizzie, we need to know how this works. Come on, you're here so tell us. Are you scared anymore?"

A hesitation. Then: "Not really."

"Why not?"

"Because I'm not scaring myself with that stupid book."

"It's not just that."

Liz nodded. "Okay. It's so weird. And I . . ."

"What?"

"I can't really remember what was so scary about the whole thing."

Rat nodded, chewed on her knuckle some. Amy grabbed a pillow for her lap, nervous, because she realized something else; the effect of the night on her. She still knew her brother and sister, remembered them—how could you let slip someone you loved so fast?—but the Rudnick twins, those kids they were talking about. They had the same name, sort of, she remembered that, but . . . she couldn't remember what they looked like.

It was like last night's dreams. Faded.

They were important, though; weren't they? Didn't the twins have something to do with this bad thing?

"I think we're in an awful lot of trouble," Amy said.

Rat's silence showed she agreed.

Liz was being cheery, though; it was all a slumber party to her now. "So who sleeps where?" she asked.

"There's the bunk," Amy said. "I'm going to sleep on the floor."

"It's your room . . ."

"I'll take the floor; I've been sleeping there all week anyway."

So she did, and eventually the room quieted down.

118

Maybe they went to sleep, maybe they never made it; it didn't matter. Amy didn't know if she was the first to awake, the first to notice, but she was wide awake searching for the ceiling in the black when she heard the noise, which at first seemed like some sort of a scratch, then fell into a pattern. . . .

There it was again; a tap on the window.

Liz sat bolt upright on the bed. "What was that?"

Amy said, "This is it."

"It? What do you mean, it?" Rat grabbed the heavy book now, saying, "I don't know what I'm going to do with this."

"If there's a giant leech out there, please hit me with it," said Liz. "I've been down this road before."

"Quiet," said Amy. The rapping on the window came again.

"What do we do?"

"Call your mom?"

"No."

"The police?"

"No, quiet." Amy tried to think.

"What are you guys worried about? The boogie man? Pull back the curtain and look," said Liz.

"No!" Amy was remembering the horrible visions she'd had of what might be out there peeking in. The Caretaker, what if it was that horrible Caretaker standing out there ready to take all of their souls away? What would the consequences of that be?

What was he?

"This is nutty, I'm going to look." Before anything else could be said Liz jumped down and peeked out the window. Next she giggled.

Giggled? No, no, here we go.

Next, as she drew open the curtains, Liz opened the window.

"Hey!" Amy jumped but it was too late. The window was open and Travis and Dave were whispering and waving in at them.

Amy laughed herself, from relief. Rat wasn't laughing, though. "What's this?" she said, waving the book.

"What do you think it is?" asked Liz. "It's a slumber party, guys crash slumber parties."

"It's not a slumber party."

"Well, it's something."

Travis stuck his head in the window; he had a sense of urgency about him, although Dave—who was standing beside him—didn't seem quite so serious. Dave seemed to be to Travis what Liz was to her and Rat; playing along, but not in a serious way. Travis said, "Hey, everybody, we need to talk at you. This is so crazy."

Rat frowned. "We're sick of that word."

"I mean because it's not crazy."

"No?"

Travis shook his head. "What you said, Amy. What you said."

"And what did I say?"

He explained. "Wally's boat is gone."

"What?"

"Who's Wally?" asked Liz.

"Never mind," said Rat.

"We went down to the beach," said Travis. "The whole boat is gone, it's like it was never there. There's no hole in the sand or anything."

"Or anything."

"It's not like you could just drag it out of there."

"Couldn't you?"

"You said this was happening."

Amy had no reply to that.

"Hey, can we come in?" asked Dave.

"No way."

"Why not? If it's life and death why not?"

"I don't know," said Amy, but she did know, although she would never admit it. Not ever. Not yet, anyway. Not admit that the feelings of fear and suspicion in her were still strong, but not as strong. She was back on the old *don't-get-Ma-angry* instinct, as opposed to the survival instinct, the worry that something of life and death was going on. As with Liz, Amy's feeling was fading.

No. No. She wouldn't let it. . . .

Amy said, "What are you guys going to do?"

"That's what we wanted to ask you."

"Who else knows about this?"

"I talked to Mike Hollingworth, Stevie Ulrich. A couple of other guys I met, but I don't think they believed me, yet. They will."

"Why do you think?"

"Because people are disappearing. Just like you said. Stacy's gone, Noonie Oleson."

"I don't want to hear this . . ." said Liz. "This is like the worst ghost story."

"It's not a ghost story," said Travis. "We need to do something."

"No, we don't need to do anything," said Amy. "The number one thing in any horror movie—"

"Why is it always the number one thing?" asked Liz. "What about the number three and four things?"

"All I know is . . ."

"Besides, I was in way more horror movies than you ever have been. I think maybe I know what to do."

Amy spun to Rat. "Is that what you think?"

"I don't know. Maybe. Maybe with the guys."

"Listen to yourselves," said Amy. "This happens in every horror movie, a bunch of kids think they can take on whatever the bad thing is. Well, it ain't happening. No way."

"Come on," said Liz. "You read that book. We know what to do, we know what we have to do."

Liz was smiling at Dave. "I know what I have to do."

"Just like in the movies," agreed Dave, grinning.

"You're all going to die. No, worse than die, you're all going away. Don't you realize that?"

"I think we'll be all right," said Travis.

"That's what you're supposed to think . . ."

Finally Amy just told them to go; dressing quickly Rat followed Liz out the window, off to who knew where, although Amy had a good enough idea.

"Aren't you coming?"

"Absolutely no way."

Amy shut the window, pulled the curtain, and shivered.

Not to worry, not worry. Dad was coming. Everything was going to be all right, just trust in the old man. He should be there the next day, no problem.

Tap-tap-tap.

They were back, rapping at the window again. Finally they'd come to their senses. Jerking open the curtain Amy started to open the window, saying, "So you guys are getting smart after all—"

She stopped, choked.

Scratching at the window, eyes heavy with the dark sorrow of ages, was her little sister Sarah. . . .

Control had the Master furious; His anger barely in control.

Correction. His anger was not in control; already He'd killed—not killed, sent for—two of His own disciples and more would have to be taken before this disaster was again under control.

"You took the little boys and the girl," He slurred to the woman who had run the post office. He had gathered those necessary for witness of the punishment to the cannery, and He slurred because He was not used to speaking, usually He communicated with His eyes, with the Great Mind, but He wanted witnesses, He wanted the others present to hear and understand.

The woman who ran the post office—an islander who looked thirty-five but was in fact almost ninety years old, thanks to His magick—should have been petrified, should have dropped to her worshipful knees, but instead she tried to lie. "I didn't."

"You did."

"Did not."

"Did so."

"Wasn't me."

What sort of sarcastic answer was that for an immortal creature to slap back with? What was He to do now? Argue? "I know it was you. I know."

123

The woman hesitated, then said, "I only did it because Billy said it would be okay."

"What?"

"She's a liar!" yelled Billy. Billy was originally the man who cared for the parks and the common and other town landmarks; now he spent a lot of time with something called Nintendo, and an ever increasing sports card collection. He stood and pointed back at the post office woman. "It was her idea. I only took one of the twins. She was only going to do one, and that was stupid, you can't leave one twin, can't—"

"Silence!"

The Greatest Mind of All Time needed a moment to clear the images, a moment to think, but now He could hear the two muttering at each other. The Great Master moved to turn on them, but was very surprised by what He saw.

"We know what we're doing," said the woman, surly now, too surly toward the Greatest Mind of All Time. "Why do you always have to boss us around all the time?"

That was the final abuse. Take them all, the madness in His brain screamed. So He did take them, both complainers, and all six witnesses before they could scramble from the cannery.

The Greatest Mind of All Time fumed.

For thirty years He practiced His own patience on Patience; He gave them immortality, and this was the thanks given Him.

When had this started? How had it happened? His vampyres were doing their own sendings, taking their own victims. Without permission, without consideration of the implications of their haphazard harvesting of the crop of young people He and the Hookman worked so hard to bring to the island each year, without waiting for the Feast. No respect for the required traditions.

No respect for anything from the Old Country.

It made little sense. In some ways these immortals of His were so much more immature than any of the young victims they had been absorbing over the years. This was insane. Had He not passed along His wisdom? Did He not teach the lessons of the immortals? Of course He had.

With Hookman's help He made the island into an immortal paradise, taking the occasional traveller or tourist, preparing the Great Feast each year, yet the disciples seemed to pay less and less attention to His instructions as the years waned, they didn't understand what was best, how He was looking after their best interests. They were irresponsible, never planning for their future, totally out of control, acting like a bunch of—

The mind of the two-thousand, seven-hundred-and-nineteen-year-old immortal became almost as chilly as the blood that ran in His veins; His wisdom slammed at high velocity into the brick wall of His logic. Oh, no. . . .

The children.

In this great instant His mistake came to Him and the Great Mind boggled; what to do? What to do?

The children. This was a shocking surprise to Him and—for the first time in centuries, He felt the nervous, sickening twitch inside his gut because for as long as He had been on the island the Master hadn't noticed. For centuries He feasted on kings and artists, great minds and tempered skills; even the scores of young people sent for on the island had done little to dilute what He was. But by granting His immortal *disciples an exclusive diet of children, by letting them absorb only children, He diluted their brains and gave their immortal bodies the souls and mentalities of children.*

No, no, no—the mistake He hadn't even realized He was making. In the Old Country He was betrayed by children, and unintentionally He had set himself up for just the same betrayal again.

Something had to be done, would be done, would be started this very night to salvage the disaster, to change the situation. Even if He had to wipe out the whole island, everyone, and summon home the Hookman to help Him build again, so be it, but there was no escaping the awful truth.

The Greatest Mind of All Time had surrounded Himself with a bunch of crazy kids. . . .

12

"Oh my God . . ."

At first Amy stepped quickly back from the window, startled, but her little sister was calling to her through the glass now, sounding very desperate. "Amy, please."

"What? Sarah . . ."

Sarah seemed to be looking around, over her shoulder, as if she expected to see something. "Hurry, let me in or they're going to get me."

"What? Who?"

"Amy, *please*, they're coming."

There was no way Amy could ignore that, the fear in her sister's voice, the shudder in the way her lips trembled as she spoke. There were tears in the terrified little girl's eyes so Amy opened the window, but Sarah didn't move.

"Amy, please . . ."

"What?"

"Tell me I can come in."

That was weird; there was something in the vampyre book about that, and Amy instantly froze. "What did you say?"

"Ask me to come in. *Please*."

Invitation; that was it. A vampyre could not cross a threshold—a door, a window, a secure property line—

127

without an invitation. That was one of the universal restrictions of magic.

Was Sarah . . . ?

No, this was her sister, her scared little sister, and not some horrible long-fanged monster who could do the fearsome thing described in the big book. "The window's open," said Amy.

"It's too hard for me. Pull me inside."

Remembering Sarah's game, Amy said, "A squirrel could crawl inside easy."

An emotion seemed to sweep across Sarah's little face; her eyes became devious. "Can I be a squirrel and crawl inside? Can I come in? Can I come in?"

Devious? How could a little girl's eyes become devious? There was no cruelty in Sarah's eyes, never, not her little sister and the more Amy looked at her little sister's eyes the more she trusted her, the more she realized it was her sister, safe and back—thank God. So Amy said, "Come inside."

A wind pushed the curtains back; Sarah didn't crawl inside, she was swept there by the wind. In one blurred motion Sarah was before Amy, only now there was something false in what she was, what she pretended to be. Not so much Sarah as an *impression* of Sarah, a slightly faded photograph. As if this was the image of Sarah now missing from the picture Ma took on the ferry.

"Oh, no . . ."

"*Saaank you.*"

"What?" Amy was thrown off balance by the voice, not her sister's but coming from within her sister, below the voice box, below the throat; the voice was deeper, a voice of soiled ages.

A horror movie voice.

Oh, no. No way. . . .

"*In Xanadu . . .*" said the voice.

Amy stumbled.

Her sister changed then; shifted as she—it—*whatever it was*—spoke. She grew, pulled taller, her skin stretching as if suddenly it was rubber, as if she were trying on a new body before Amy's very eyes and perhaps she was, because the creature that had been her sister was suddenly taller and still as close to Amy as before, except the face was now pulling into a man's face, and older, but not so old; he was a movie star, or could have been. He was gorgeous, perhaps the most handsome man Amy had ever seen in her life, and that included on TV and in the movies. She actually trembled at the sight of him, the twitch of his smile, the excitement—the fire, the energy!—in his eyes. If only he would reach out or something, touch her hand maybe, please maybe try and kiss her—

No! Amy jumped back, but it was too late. She remembered the warnings from *Vampyres* but it was too late. She was alone with him, and she had twice lost herself in his eyes.

The eyes are truly the window to the soul; the unguarded ramparts from which one views and is viewed by the world. Eyes see only truth, even if all that seems visible is lies. And it is through the eyes that the Vampyre hunts; through the eyes that He shall possess you. . . .

He? She? It? Whatever he was, he smiled, speaking, except he spoke in verse—a poem:

> *In Xanadu did Kubla Khan*
> *A stately pleasure-dome decree:*
> *Where Alph, the sacred river, ran*
> *Through caverns measureless to man*
> *Down to a sunless sea. . . .*

129

Amy whispered. "Alph?"

"Do you know Coleridge?"

"What?"

"Samuel Taylor Coleridge," said the thing that had been her sister, speaking much more clearly now. "Nineteenth-century English poet and opium addict. Had I been disposed I should have enjoyed corresponding with him—you miss so much trapped in a watery grave. But the centuries passed me by, just like they did Coleridge. Pity. Immortal as I am, I've been denied so much of my time, my own history. The past is as dead to me as it is to you.

"I respect your courage," the thing went on, stretching out His hands and nails now. They were long, growing. Claws. The lines on His face were sharper now, more clear, more real. The longer she was with Him, the more in focus He seemed. Masks off, thought Amy.

So be it. "Who are you?" She swallowed, but found it easier to speak.

"Not *what* am I? I also respect your class, Ms. Meyer. As well as your upbringing. I'm not surprised, of course; you have the breeding, but still . . ."

"What?"

"Nothing. Just still."

He stared at Amy a long moment, and she asked, "Who are you?"

"*Conversation,*" said the thing, as if savoring a delicious morsel of food. He—It—paced the room. "My intention, of course, was to send for you immediately, begin to put to rest this wretched nonsense that has grown so far out of control, but good conversation is so rare. Especially on this island. So much to be treasured."

130

"What?"

"I respect your mind. Does that surprise you so much?"

"No." And that was true; for some reason it didn't surprise her.

The thing—He—seemed pleased with her reaction. "*Excellent*, so excellent. I almost wish I could spare you for one of my disciples; I know one or two who could use some of what you are. Alas."

"Alas?"

"Such an opportunity does not present itself this evening."

"Who are you?"

"The same repeated question, but I owe you that much perhaps. After all, escape being no longer possible—surely you feel my power over you by now."

"No." Except that wasn't true; she felt something. A numbness, not in her body. In her. . . .

"We are becoming one; your will is already simply mine. You can't even run from me."

"No."

"Oh, yes. Try and escape."

"I don't want to."

"Exactly," said the creature.

"You're a vampyre."

There. It was said, just like in every horror movie, just like it was Liz saying in her dramatic scream *you're a giant slug*, only it was Amy, and this was really happening. Wasn't it?

"I'm afraid so," said the vampyre. "Yes."

Amy watched him a long moment, feeling very timid, but very curious. "Is . . . is this the way you really look? Are you really so . . ."

"Attractive? I'm not even sure, I've long debated whether or not my appearance was by evolution or

131

choice, chance or affectation. I draw you to me, do I not?"

Blushing, Amy asked, "And that's why I don't want to leave you? Because of your powers?"

He nodded. "It's almost worthy of an apology, but would a spider apologize for its web? Does a frog apologize for evolution's gift of a long sticky tongue? Magick—*maj-eeck*—is simply part of nature's way."

Amy didn't know what to say. She felt no fear, only intense curiosity—and perhaps a strange longing—but nothing like the nervous, stomach-cramping fear of before. Her friends were off on some weird stupid excursion, but she was learning. She was learning things which were true. Not necessarily good, but they were true.

"I ramble," He said. *He was so beautiful, though; let Him ramble the night away.* She sat enthralled. "I lecture; it is my nature, as you'll discover. It's my way. Do you really want to know who I am, as opposed to simply *what* I am?"

"Yes. Oh, yes. Please, I mean." Was this how it happened? A now distant part of Amy's mind was asking if this was what happened to Sarah, to the others who were now gone forever. *Was the same thing happening now?* Would Liz and Rat and Travis and the others simply discover that she was another victim no adult could recall a thing about? Would Dad arrive to find Ma and none of her children, with Ma totally unconcerned about the empty house she was staying in?

"My name is Tevas Endres," said the vampyre.

"Tevas? That's a weird name."

"Don't try to understand; it's from an age before yours. I am nearly three thousand years old, and I possess wisdom and intelligence far beyond your comprehension. At least for now."

"What do you mean, for now?"

The vampyre took her hand; she expected cold, but it felt so warm. *Tevas Endres*. He said, soothingly, so soothingly, "Well . . . I must send for you soon. Which means we'll be together always, you'll be with your sister; of course, all of this shall be subjugation."

"I don't understand."

"Subject. Your being, subject to my will. Incorporated as a small part of what I am."

Unable to even move to back away, and not really wishing to, Amy said, "I still don't understand."

"Nor should you. Simply understood, all of what you are shall become a small part of me, like one bee in a hive. Which is not so bad as extinction? You shall be immortal, Amy; consider that."

"I don't want to be immortal."

"But you shall. Immortality is glorious."

"You killed my sister."

"Not I; she was sent for by another, and I sent for the other in punishment; the creature which took your sister disobeyed, did it on her own, but she, too, is gone. But don't think your sister is dead. She's not, she's immortal—in me. All that she was, her memories, her emotions, herself; all of that lives on in me. She is part of me now, part of me."

"No . . ."

"Just as you shall be."

"I'm not ready."

"Not that I haven't made my mistakes over the years; I have. Surrounding myself with disciples, that was a mistake. I fancied it a marvelous idea once, but never before by tradition had any of my kind

133

created more than one or two allies; I gave life to nearly a hundred. A hundred vampyre slaves. Only I lost control."

"I don't want this to happen."

"You will soon enough, and my problem shall become your dilemma; you seem a sharp mind, perhaps we'll solve it together. You the element, me the Master. Perhaps we'll make the answer . . ."

The vampyre, Tevas Endres, the Master, stood now, still holding Amy's hand, engulfing her helplessly into His eyes, and He would have had her then, consumed every bit, everything that was her, had not the unexpected occurred.

The trembling.

The sudden shocks.

Except they did not come from Amy, as might be expected—they came from the Master, who was caught by surprise by the sudden loss of control over even this, His own immortal body. His legs collapsed beneath Him, and He fell into a spasm, and even as He dropped and shuddered Amy recognized what was happening to Him.

A seizure! An epileptic seizure!

Sarah's seizures! This thing, the Master, He had taken all that Sarah was—consumed and become her— and now He was having one of her seizures!

What happened next would have been beyond the comprehension of any islander.

The Master Himself lost control.

Centuries of imprisonment beneath the sea—an age where He could not move Himself, where He was forced to await the disposition of shifting seabed and churning storm—these were nothing. What was happening to Him now was . . . was. . . .

It was as if He were being sent for, as if someone else was consuming Him, subjugating Him. . . .

He was going away, being pushed deep into Himself, no coherent thoughts, nothing now, the spasms, the jerks, the total loss of control. For the first time since the Pharaohs ruled Egypt, He was afraid, He was very afraid. . . .

13

When the vampyre recovered enough to raise His eyes to Amy, He was gone; Amy was with Sarah again.

Oh my God. . . .

Startled, Amy backed away, but it *was* Sarah, speaking in her true voice now, reaching out for Amy's hand in a different way, gently, not the grasp of the vampyre. Sarah said, "Sissy . . ."

"Oh, God. . . ."

The little girl closed her eyes, then opened them, reaching to touch her own face. Then she took a deep breath, and sighed. "Sissy. . . ."

This is it, thought Amy; her father hadn't raced to her rescue in time and now she was losing her mind. Vampyres were prone to epileptic fits and young girls suffered nervous breakdowns. She was tough, she held on, but she couldn't hold on long enough.

"Sissy . . ."

"What?"

"Run."

Run? "What are you talking about?"

"You have to run, Sissy; run away."

The pain in little Sarah's face was so true now, so real that Amy felt her heart breaking even as she slipped to her own knees. "What can I do for you?"

Sarah shook her head, slowly. She seemed so much

older now, her voice so much wiser than it had ever been before. "There's nothing you can do, Sissy. I'm just a mask now. Just a part of Him, but so much more."

Staring in shock, Amy didn't speak. Just waited.

Sarah went on, saying, "I can see things—I know things."

"You're free now. You're Sarah again."

"No. I'm just a mask."

"How can you . . ."

"He never takes the weak." Sarah explained it all, there in the dark of the room. "He never devours the sick, because if He does, *He'll* become weak and sick. That's why old Lenore gets to wander around the island pushing her shopping cart."

Old Lenore? *Michael, Michael, I remember Michael.* Yes! Amy remembered.

"Lenore knows," said Sarah. "She *knows*, but nothing could happen to her because she's sick in the head. And the vampyres don't want to be sick in the head."

"But . . ."

Sarah nodded, the joke not so private. "He didn't know about me, because it was the pharmacy lady who took me, and He got her in revenge—and got me. He told them not to take anyone. Except He didn't know about my epilepsy, and now He's stuck with it—it's *His* epilepsy." Sarah smiled for the first time.

"What?"

"He feeds them children, Sissy, but only at the Great Feast, and that's Saturday night, during the full moon. It's an Old Country tradition, from the old times. Only He can't wait now, too much is happening. His people wouldn't listen to Him, and they started taking kids too soon and you and some others started seeing what was happening—"

"Others?"

"Yes," said Sarah, her eyes so blank as she spoke. "There are others who know. But the Master is sending them away soon. He's sending everyone away."

"No . . ."

"He's been around for so long but . . . there's no time, He'll be back when the spasm passes; I'll bet He's going to be surprised." Sarah smiled again.

"I don't want to leave you."

"If you don't run now you won't be able to. He has the power. It can't be beaten, Sissy; the world gave it to Him."

"The world?"

"The *magick* of the world."

"No . . ."

"Please, go away."

"What about Dad? He's coming, he can help. I have a book on vampyres, I've been reading it and I—"

"No. Go away, beware the Hookman."

"What?" What did she mean?

"Beware the Hookman. He's not a friend, Sissy."

"Hookman?" Did she mean the Hookman of the stories from the beach party? "Sarah, you don't mean . . ."

"The Hookman is bad, and he won't tell you stories first like the vampyre does; he won't take and make you immortal. He just hurts you."

"What?"

"He just kills you."

"What? No, wait, talk to me baby, please . . ."

Sarah couldn't speak, couldn't talk; her little neck muscles were pulling tight now and her eyes rolling back, although she was fighting it. "Run, please . . ."

It was happening, Amy knew it. In a moment Sarah would be gone and the vampyre would return and this time Amy knew there would be no hesitation; this time He would strike and she would be taken in an instant, pleasantly or not it would be over, and it was that that sent Amy jumping through the window, into the sand outside and running down the beach.

Where to go? What to do? She was in her bare feet, stumbling across rock and twig and sand and she stumbled in the direction of the beach party, where the beach party always was, but she didn't expect anything to be there; it was late. Not that she expected to make it, anyway; there was a vampyre behind her, after all; she could hear that shriek once again, the horrible sound which she had heard that night with the police lady:

"Arrrrrrraaaaaaaaggggghhhh!"

Him, it had to be Him; was He like the creatures in the book *Vampyres*? Could He transform Himself into a wolf, or a bat? Was He running her down even now, concealed in the guise of some horrible beast?

Where was she going? What did she think she was going to do?

Ma. She had to find Ma—who was out at some function with Katie at the Kensit School, some mother-daughter thing. Even if her mother was caught up in the whirlwind nonsense that affected so many, even if Ma and Katie were inadvertent bad guys, she didn't want to let them walk in on a life-sucking vampyre. Or did she?

But how was she going to stay alive herself? Protect herself? And what about Rat, Liz, and the others who were just be-bopping around in the night trying to play hero? Where did they get off to?

"Aaaaaaaaaaaaaaaggggggggggghhhhhh!" The cry from the night came again, and Amy shuddered.

139

She started running as fast as she could toward the Kensit School.

The function at the school was a sort of mixer-get together, and it was being held in the only place Kensit apparently held things, the auditorium hall of the main building. Amy found it by the noise and the lights, wondering all the way if she was being stalked by something she couldn't handle.

Of course this made sense—another number one thing from horror movies was the fact that the hero usually wound up alone. Did this make her the hero? Why? She was the one fighting hardest *not* to have to be the hero.

There was nobody watching the door and Amy got in; conversations and small talk were going on all over the place. Katie was nowhere to be seen, but Ma was caught up with that Ms. Knoll, the fat counselor from the family session. They both smiled at Amy's appearance, but Ma looked a little confused. "Didn't he find you?"

Amy's heart nearly stopped. "Who? What? What are you talking about?"

"Your father. He was just here, looking for you. I sent him up to the bungalow with Katie."

"He's here?" Didn't he say that Amy had called him?

"Yes, he said he got a break from his appointments for a few days and decided to come out for a while. I thought for sure they'd meet you at the house."

The screams, Amy thought then. *No, that couldn't be. But what if the screams were Daddy and Katie confronting the vampyre?*

Oh, my God. . . .

"I have to go," said Amy, backing away.

140

"Ride up with me," said Ma. "I'm leaving in a minute."

"Can't," said Amy, noticing then that some of the adults in the auditorium were watching her a bit more closely than they maybe should have been. *Islanders.* "I've got to . . . I've got to go . . ."

Amy ran out of the building, off of the school grounds, panting and sweating and wondering just how much of a nightmare was going on, and how much of it she was responsible for? After all, she'd violated so many of the horror movie rules, and now look what was happening.

"Girl!"

The hands had her and Amy screamed and squirmed, but there was no point; He was too strong and He had her, *it was over*, except it wasn't the vampyre she was seeing.

It was the bone white face of the Caretaker.

"What's going on? Hey, there's Amy!"

There was another beach party going on—or maybe the same party, maybe the party never really stopped—and the party was in the shadow of the dragon, the dark shadow of the cannery. Except this time the Caretaker was her savior, and not the thing of nightmares.

Amy wanted to go home—had no choice but to try—except the Caretaker wouldn't go that way; he led her toward the fire and crowd of the beach party and left her there, saying only, "This is a bad night. This is a very bad night."

Amy said nothing, just looked around. Her mind was half-gone anyway, she decided; roll with it.

Things had changed, though, even with the partiers; that was easy to see. There were no more than half the kids who had been there before.

"You look like hell," said Liz, suddenly appearing beside her and handing Amy a purse.

"What's going on?" Overexcited, Amy blurted it out. "Where is everybody? He was there, I mean *He* came for me. The vampyre."

"The vampyre?"

"One of them, there are lots of them. I don't know what to do, my dad's here somewhere. I've got to go home."

"Everybody's here, we'll go together. Take the purse, take the brush and a mirror, fix yourself."

Swallowing, Amy took a breath and nodded. "This is yours?"

"No, it's Rat's. I can't find mine, it's somewhere."

Composing herself, Amy watched the shuffling Caretaker leave the campfire; he was walking away, down toward the pier, the dark pier at the foot of the dragon.

The dragon. The huge black cannery standing above them. Was it a coincidence that they were here, now, tonight? Was it just chance that this big beach party took place so close to that place?

That was when the girl islander came then—Kelly, the girl from the first party, the creepy one who Amy *knew* was one of *them*. Kelly touched Amy's hand; her touch was ice and her breath sweet onions. "Why are you doing this?" asked Kelly.

"What?"

"I know all of what you're doing. Everybody does. Everybody is smarter than you think they are, Amy. Nobody's mean and bloody and that's why you can walk around at night when maybe you shouldn't be able to, but everybody is still smarter than you are." Kelly smiled, just another smug all-powerful vampyre cheerleader type with lots of money and eternal life.

Terrific; *an immortal creep.* Amy trembled, and said, "What are you?"

Kelly shrugged, pursed her lips and said, "You could be one of us. You don't have to die or go away. You could be like me. I'm going to live forever."

"Big deal, you're going to be fifteen forever. Who wants that?"

"Maybe *you* do," said Kelly. "I have powers beyond anything you'll ever know. I could show you."

Reaching into Rat's purse, Amy said, "No, I'll show you . . ."

Amy flashed the mirror—holding the reflecting glass to Kelly's face off the light of the fire. The cold girl gave an involuntary yelp and twisted away.

"What do you see?" asked Amy.

"Nothing."

"Go on, look, if you're so tough." Amy shoved the glass closer and the sudden movement made Kelly stumble backward; she lost her balance and pulled herself back together.

"What do you see?"

"I don't see anything."

"You know what you see. You know what you see."

"Amy. *Wait.*"

Now Amy jumped, turning quickly.

It was her father, standing there on the beach beside her, out of breath and looking confused and anxious.

It was her father; thank God. It was Daddy.

14

"Daddy!"

Rushing to her father who stood very nearby now, Amy threw her arms around him and hugged for dear life; he hugged back as best he could. His face was calm, reassuring. "Easy, easy, everything is going to be all right."

"Is it? Is it all going to be all right?"

"Easy, baby."

Katie was with Daddy and she just sort of shrugged the whole thing off, unimpressed—she wandered over to join the party, saying something under her breath. Liz was back now, with Rat, Travis, and Dave in tow, and they had a lot to say but Amy waved for them to be quiet. The four of them were nowhere near as serious looking as they had been disappearing into the night, though; they all held soft drinks—even brought one for Amy, but she turned it down. "My dad's here," she said.

"So what's the deal?" asked Liz.

"What's the *deal*? The deal—"

Amy stopped talking.

Amy was nervous now, suddenly chilled, because for a second—for just a second—she had been so happy to see her father, that she forgot why she was so happy. Something was wrong, somebody important was missing—

"Sarah," she blurted, saying it fast so she wouldn't forget it. "Sarah, Sarah, I remember Sarah."

Michael, Michael, I remember Michael. . . .

The same thing was starting to happen to her, the forgetting. How could she forget? "I was attacked by a vampyre," she said out loud. *That* was it.

"A what?"

"You know, you guys know."

"We all do," said Daddy, nodding; the most serious of the bunch; it was as if he was confessing a great secret. "We all know what's happening now."

"Do we?" This was from Liz. "I'm glad somebody does."

"Quiet," said Rat. Travis just listened.

Looking around at the others, Amy shivered. "Let's get out of here."

"In a minute. There're things to do."

"Things to do?"

"Definitely." Easing back from her father, Amy looked around, trying to figure out what he was talking about, or better yet what he intended to do.

"What's going on here isn't normal. It's supernatural. *Magick.*"

"I know," said Amy. "*We* know. Or at least we used to; I don't understand what anybody else believes anymore. I just didn't think anyone would believe me."

"I believe you all," he said. Pointing toward the great sleeping black dragon—the cannery—her father said, "There's the source. That's what you feel, what you don't understand. That's where it all comes from. That's why I'm here now."

"But what? How do you know?"

Her father explained. "Remember what you told

145

me? About what was happening? I used to spend my summers on this island."

"You did?"

"Yeah." He nodded. "With my mom and dad. We weren't islanders or anything, but we came here every summer. Things were happening even then, things I didn't understand—nobody understood."

Amy didn't understand, and she said so. "But if you thought spooky things were afoot. . . . Then why would you have us come here?"

"Maybe he wanted to get rid of you all," suggested Liz. Rat gave her a quick elbow.

"No," said her father. "There're things you don't understand." He seemed to give things a long thought, walking amidst the campfire scene. Kelly was gone, off somewhere. *Good.* Liz and Rat followed along, though. And Travis and Dave. They were more alert now, seeming to shake some of the slumber which was seizing them up. "Okay, so there's weirdness. So what are we going to do?" asked Travis.

"Nothing," said Amy, speaking for her father. "We're going to get out of here. Get off this island."

"No," said Daddy. "That won't work. That won't change anything. The bad things will still be here, on this island, in that cannery, striking out at others."

"But we have to go," said Amy, explaining herself for the first time. She felt desperate, almost ready to—for the first time—completely fall apart in front of everybody. "I come down here, and it's all just one big horror movie scene—all we need now is a bunch of torches and we're off to storm monster castle. We're not going to really do that, are we?"

"I think we have to."

"I can't. My mind won't be able to handle it."

Amy's father sighed, then stood up on a rock and tried to explain it to her, to all of them. "I know what this thing is, this *vampyre*, this consumer, the eater of souls, He takes not just the blood, but the life. Remember: The blood is the life, but the life is the blood. The very existence of its victims. Once consumed, it's as if you never existed, and the magick of the world washes you away like scrawled words in sand when the surf roars in."

"No. . . ."

"Yes. Because there's something only a few realize. All the universe is sea, *fluid*, even that part of the world with air, that part of reality we deal with each day. There is *magick*, magick is like electricity, it's one of the great mysteries that make the universe work; the engine of the world. And as with electricity, there is static magic, arc magic, tingly things—and really heavy, killer current."

"Oh my God . . ." said Rat.

"What?" Amy turned to her, hoping Rat would change sides now, choose retreat just like she wanted.

Rat didn't; she had ideas of her own now. "That all makes sense now. The stake and all that, with the vampyres."

"What?"

"We were reading in the book, it's in all the movies. Think about it. Stakes through the heart kill vampyres. Why would they? Unless magic—"

"*Magick*," corrected Amy's father.

Liz nodded. "If *magick* is the connection. Oh, God, think about it, electricity, magick, stakes through the heart—it's like grounding out a current! It must be that if the vampyre can be grounded into the earth, he's fried."

"Just like me on the roof, with the TV antenna," said Amy, remembering the first day, when she met Travis. She looked to him now.

"Yeah," Travis said, nodding very thoughtfully. "Just like if I hadn't stopped you."

"You guys cannot be serious," said Liz. "You're going to go up to the cannery, drag whoever's living in there out of a closet or something and drive a stake through his heart?"

"Doesn't have to be the heart," said Rat. "Not if grounding is the thing."

"Yeah," agreed Travis. "Any part of his body to the earth will short circuit the whole thing out. You could put it through his foot."

"But that's murder, you just can't kill somebody. You don't have any proof of anything."

"There's never going to be any proof," said Rat. "Not if the memories are taken."

"What about them?" asked Amy, pointing up at the beach, toward the town, where the islanders lived. Or *habitated*, if lived wasn't the right word.

"They come last," said Amy's father. "If this is all what we think it is, we get the head and the body will die. There're tools in that work shed, though. Things we might need. And I've got some flashlight lanterns in my jeep."

"Things we might need? Like a hammer or two?"

"Yes."

"What happens to the devoured souls, though? Are they lost forever? Have they always been? What about Sarah, Brian, Stacy, the twins, the others?"

That's something they didn't want to think about. Rat shrugged, pulling her purse together and moving to gather the things they'd need to properly explore the cannery. "If nothing else, they'll be at peace, and

148

not part of some horrible monster, living like that forever."

"Are we all going?" asked Travis. He was about to make a crack about girls not being up to it, or at least that's what Amy was hoping; this time she'd take him up on it. Except he didn't, and besides— Dad was here.

"No," said Dad. Instructing Dave he said, "You need to get to a telephone. Tell the police what we're doing and wait for them." He called over to Katie to give her the same instructions.

"No way," said Dave. "I want to go up to the cannery with you guys."

"You'll see it all soon enough. If nobody makes the call who knows what could happen? We're depending on you."

Dave reluctantly nodded.

So they started walking, the five of them, just like the stars of every horror movie Amy ever saw and overanalyzed, but at least her father was with her, at least there was some sort of an anchor to this madness; even Rat agreed. "Your dad seems super cool," she said.

"Yeah, he'll handle things for us."

"What's wrong with his arm, though?"

Amy explained, an explanation she'd made many, many times over the years and to various friends. "It's not his arm, it's his hand. He got it cut off in an accident years ago, so he has to wear that artificial one. It's not so bad to look at now; before it was a lot worse. He used to wear a hook . . ."

They brought Him the news negligently late, of course; the Master had already sensed it before the man who ran the docks rushed the information to the chamber. "He's here, Hookman is here."

Excellent, thought the Greatest Mind in the World. Perhaps this nonsense will be done and away now. Perhaps some semblance of control could be reestablished over the domain of Cyder Island. There was a lot to do, many would need to be sent for—something would need be done about this new thing, this new terror in His brain. That blasted little girl! Betrayed by a child once more.

But never again. All family business would be concluded soon enough, there would be control and the torments would be gone, life reordered.

The disciple's question was stupid and foolish, as always. "Shall I send for Hook? Tell him you need—"

"Do nothing. Hookman will bring himself before me."

The disciple nodded, and the Master explained Himself, even though He need explain to no one. "I belonged to him even before he belonged to me . . ."

15

Shrouded in darkness, the dragon slept, and although Amy was wary of waking the creature—the dragon of her nightmares—she followed as her father led them on, up the hill toward the cannery.

They passed through the black gate easily enough; Amy's father grabbed a nearby brick and smashed the cheap lock fastening the link chain holding it shut. Crossing the cracked concrete of the grounds, Amy felt a chill in the wind; thick patches of weeds grew everywhere, and the occasional small animal scampered away. Until they started talking the only other sound was the crashing of the surf, so very close by.

"I used to play around here as a kid," her father said, the first to speak.

"There're supposed to be a lot of stories about the cannery," said Travis.

"There are. I told most of them."

"Yeah?"

"Yeah," said her father.

"So what are we going to do if we find anything? That's what I want to know," said Liz. She held the flashlight they had picked up on the way up and shined the light in her own face, bleaching her face white in its glow.

"I thought you didn't believe anymore."

"I don't know. Maybe I do. How can I tell? For all I know this is some setup of my Uncle's, maybe he's filming me right now."

"He *should* be filming," agreed Rat. "This would make some weird movie."

"This way, I think," said Daddy.

"Down and dark, that makes sense," agreed Travis.

Liz and Rat were more nervous, but followed, with Rat making a running commentary of the dampness as they crept down some catwalk stairs, following the flickering, overlapping flashlight beams. "What makes more sense is this thing living with the rats and bugs and who knows what else."

"He has powers to command lower things," explained Amy's father. "When He is strong they act from His strength."

"Wonderful."

Amy frowned, wondering. Wondering what she was really wondering, because how did Daddy know all of this? Why did he know all of this?

Had he been reading the book *Vampyres*, too? Why would he?

Fumbling in her purse, Rat produced the mirror again, the one Amy had used to terrify Kelly. "This and the stakes to ground out the bad guys. We aren't exactly well prepared, are we?"

"We're very prepared," said Amy's father.

They ventured down a passageway, illuminated only by hanging lanterns, glowing dim because their flames had been lowered to the lowest wick possible to keep them burning. "Who set these?" wondered Liz.

"Probably Caretaker," said Travis.

"Why don't they just use electricity?"

"They can't," answered Amy's father.

"Didn't pay their bill?"

152

"Overlapping magic," he explained. "Electricity is just another form of magic, or *magick*. *Maj-eeck*. Here the concentration of magick is so strong it overwhelms all others. Here the vampyre makes His own rules, this is His realm."

"Then why are we going down here?"

"Because this journey has to be made," answered Amy's father.

"Why?"

"Because I've been making this trip all of my life . . ."

They came to the end of the passageway, stopping just before two large wooden doors which were labeled CENTRAL RECEIVING. From the old cannery days. A row of black, corroded, and ancient lockers lined the wall, and Amy's father paused by one and pulled open the door, as if he knew what he was looking for.

"What are you doing?" Travis asked the question but even Amy was curious.

"I'm going to show you guys a neat trick," said her father. Standing before the ancient locker, he uncuffed and rolled up the sleeve of his right arm, exposing his prosthetic hand. His arm fit into the cuff at the wrist, and several elastic straps secured it at the wrist, elbow, and shoulder.

Daddy unsnapped these now.

He slid off the hand, placed it carefully in the dark locker. From inside he pulled something heavy, and shiny. It too had a cuff and straps.

It was a hook, a double hook that curved but joined together like pincers. It could be used to lift things, to hold and pick them up—normally. Except this particular hook looked modified, sharpened.

153

A snapping razor, gleaming in the flickering light.

He slipped it on in seconds, working the pincers by skilled flexing of his shoulder and elbow. The pincer blades of the hook slapped together, and Amy's father turned back to them all, smiling.

"What's going on?" asked Travis.

"The plan was to find the magick."

"Yes."

"That won't be necessary."

"What? Why not?"

"Well, I've got some excellent news for you all," said Amy's father, the Hookman. "The Master will see you now . . ."

The Master was conducting a desperate council when his old ally, the Hookman, brought the children into the chamber to stand before Him. The vampyre appeared ancient as He sat above three of his disciples, three islanders from town, all confident and questioning but now—on the appearance of the Hookman—very nervous. The Master was no longer the handsome movie star of Amy's room, not the man who had changed to little sister Sarah and back, except there was something oddly majestic about the way He sat on His chair.

No, not chair. His *throne*. Everyone was silent as they entered, and the Master's eyes followed them. No, not true. The Master's eyes followed Amy. . . .

"Wow . . ." Rat couldn't help but whisper as they were ushered into the chamber by the Hookman. Amy agreed, reaching to squeeze her friend's hand. Liz and Travis just looked nervous.

Structurally, the room they were in now was no different than any other in the ancient cannery; there was no electricity, it was lit only by kerosene lamps, the same sort of lanterns any camper might take with him to the north woods. The furnishings, however, were spectacular; a combination of luxury and history. Thick rugs, wall tapestries, paintings. Decades of work had gone into making this fish cannery room into a court; the dragon cannery was like a great black castle after all.

Amy swallowed. The furniture from the sixteenth, seventeenth, and eighteenth centuries; there was nothing modern, especially not the throne from which the Master glared down at them, especially Amy. She saw now that His ancient face shifted and bubbled, a boiling pot of emotions and wisdom; His appearance shapeshifted from one second to the next, like a hologram picture whose image changed with varying light.

The vampyre nodded from His perch. "Again we speak."

Amy heard her father answer in a way she had never heard him speak before. "My Master," he said.

"Yes," said the vampyre.

"As the blood is the life, so the life is the will to be it. To be *It*. I bring you the answer to our problems. I'm sorry for so much of the troubles."

"You aren't the trouble, Hookman. Nor are these children, really. The error, the original sin was mine." Looking over toward Amy the vampyre rose from his throne, announcing, "I am Tevas Endres, the last of my kind. And I know truths, many truths."

He was quoting again, another poem, another Coleridge poem, Amy assumed:

> *The pang, the curse, with which they died,*
> *Had never passed away:*
> *I could not draw my eyes from theirs,*
> *Nor turn them up to pray.*

155

"Nor," He added after a pause, "can I turn my eyes from yours. Any of yours."

Stepping down, Tevas Endres—the Master—the Greatest Mind in the World—walked over to where Amy stood. "Shall we study some more poetry together? I'm sure I'll be fine now. The seizure days are behind me, if I can trust the fool slave pharmacist I've taken."

"Taken?"

"Inside of me. Part of me." Tevas Endres smiled.

The vampyre made his decision. "We shall have to rid ourselves of all of them. All the children, all the adults. This is my edict: The island itself must be cleansed this very night."

"We can't possibly absorb that many people over a weekend; you know that." This was from one of the Master's disciples, the islander Mr. Haney; he sounded concerned.

"The word is not *absorb*," said the Master, frustrated—as always of late—with the general lack of respect. "We *send* for others."

"I always called it the big squeeze," said the old woman who ran the grocery.

" 'Wash 'em away' was how I put it," said the woman police chief, the third waiting disciple.

" 'Food bait'," said Haney.

"Enough, *whatever*," said the Master. "Whoever cannot be sent for must simply be killed. You do remember how to kill, don't you?"

The group muttered in the affirmative, but Haney—apparently the leader—said, "We'll need help, though."

"You wish the Hookman to help you?"

"No. We . . . I mean . . ."

156

"Very well, very well. Take those children here, make them one of you and have them help you with the bodies as well. There will be too much to dispose of, anyway."

"Thank you, Master."

The vampyre disciples came over, grabbing Travis and Amy and Liz and, almost as an afterthought, Rat, but the Hookman said, "Not Amy." So they left her, Rat turning and meeting Amy's eyes with a terrified gaze.

"Don't, you can't," said Amy.

Shaking his head, Amy's father said, "They're not going to kill them, they need them. They're going to be helpers."

"Helpers?"

Leading Rat away, the vampyre slaves said, "Come on, child, you want to live forever?" Laughing, they dragged her off, along with the others, slamming the heavy door behind them.

"No," said Amy, stepping forward. "What happened to the mystery? What happened to the magic?"

"*Magick*."

"Whatever, you can't just kill a bunch of people . . ."

"No," said Amy's father, the Hookman. "The Master would never do such, for the life is His blood. But I can . . ."

Daddy clicked his shiny metal hook; two hooks snapping and clicked together as her father raised his arm over his head.

"Daddy . . ."

"What would you have me do?" asked the Hookman.

"Help us."

"I'm sorry, Amy. There's nothing I can do for you." Taking her arm with his good hand, her father pulled Amy back, snap-snapping as they approached the shadows.

"I'll try to be fast. I'll make it so it doesn't hurt."

"What?"

"You don't want this. You can't want this. Look around you, honey."

"Daddy . . ."

"How can you call me *Daddy*?" asked the Hookman, her *father*. "Don't you realize what I really am?"

"This isn't happening," said Amy, singsonging to herself now. "This isn't happening. It isn't happening."

"I'm sorry, baby," said her father, the Hookman, closer now, beside her now. "It is."

With that he pulled Amy to her feet, but hesitated.

"Daddy . . ."

"Prepare yourself."

This isn't happening! This cannot be happening! No!

The Voice from the shadow of the throne rumbled. *"And God told Abraham to take his favorite son to the top of the mountain and slay him in sacrifice . . ."*

"Yes, Master."

"Only He stayed Abraham's knife just in time."

"Yes."

"Would you expect me to stay your hook?"

"No."

"Very well, then. Your favorite child awaits."

Tears on her cheeks, Amy looked at her father, the Hookman, and asked, "Daddy, how can you do this?"

"I should have done this long ago. It would have been easier."

"Easier?"

"Yes. I shouldn't have had children." There were tears in his eyes now, in her father's eyes, in the Hookman's eyes. "I'm an animal, Amy. *A murderer.* I've done this before. All the time. I've killed so, so often. I've got the madness in me, you do, too. Katie does. Sarah did, Brian, too; I thought that the Master could take you away and I wouldn't have to do anything, wouldn't have to remember anything, but the *magick* doesn't work for me."

"It *shall* work for you," said the Master. "This very night you shall become immortal."

"Everyone on the island is going away tonight," said the Hookman. "Or dying. I don't know which is best. Goodbye, Amy."

"No!"

"Goodbye."

He turned Amy now so she couldn't look at his face, could not make an appeal with her eyes, and Amy felt his hand move behind her, the razor hook close to her throat, and then she felt the violent *whump* as she was twisted and thrown to the ground.

No, no, no, Amy's mind whimpered, her heart pounding. Was she dying now? Her throat cut? It didn't hurt, not at all.

It didn't hurt because she wasn't cut. Rolling to her knees, Amy saw that her father, the Hookman, was caught, in a fight with another dark figure beneath the amber glow of the lamps. The *Caretaker*!

"Leave her alone," said the Caretaker, shoving Hookman flat against the greasy wall. "Leave the little girl alone!" The hook swung sharp now, slicing Caretaker's face but the old man didn't scream; he just gritted his teeth together and held on, dragging the killer along.

The hook swung wildly again, only this time it smashed into one of the kerosene lamps; oil and flame exploded out, splashing both men, setting them both alight.

Only the Hookman screamed. "Noooooooooo!"

Amy pulled herself free from the rope coils now and stumbled forward toward the light, toward the flames; both men were totally engulfed by the fire now, she could see Caretaker's face boiling but although they stumbled together he did not release his iron grip; he and Hookman crashed down now, through the floorboards and down into the sea.

Amy stood there. Stood there until she realized she wasn't alone, the vampyre was beside her now.

"He was my favorite," said the Master.

"He . . . he was my daddy," said Amy, shivering and shuddering, still unable to believe what she had seen, what she saw with her own eyes. *It couldn't be true! None of this could be true!*

"You're strong, so strong," said the vampyre.

Tripping away, Amy felt her back against the wall. No more room to run, except the dropped bag was there on the floor, open, and she pulled out the mirror—except it was broken.

Tevas was approaching her now and Amy did the only thing she could—she held the broken mirror up at Him.

He hesitated, looking away. He did not flee, though; He said, "There is no image there, the reflecting glass is too shattered to decipher."

"You *know* what's in there," said Amy.

Again Tevas paused, but did not retreat. Appearing to summon back His strength, the vampyre said, "You're not like the others, not so much a child. I could consume you myself. We could be together.

You, too, could know the wisdom of the ages. Ancient Egypt, the Greeks, the gods; Camelot. The musicians and artists of the Old Country . . ."

Tevas was speaking quietly now, taking control of her eyes, and too late Amy realized again that it was happening. That He had her. That He survived. That He always survived.

It was a mental thing, almost—yes—telepathy, because He was inside her mind now, they were nearly as one, and He told her the poem again, the Coleridge poem, as He pulled her so much closer to what He was:

> *The many men, so beautiful!*
> *And they all dead did lie:*
> *And a thousand, thousand slimy things*
> *Lived on; and so did I. . . .*

He pulled Amy close to Him now, his nails—claws now, digging into her back—caressing her, His lips moving to touch her, consume her, take her—

No!

He jolted, stood suddenly straight.

The mind of Tevas Endres raged: Another convulsion? Another seizure? Now?

No! Tevas was shuddering and convulsing now, but it wasn't epilepsy, it was an old iron fish lance sticking from his back, and an iron link chain connecting the lance to the concrete floor of the cannery. And Amy was forcing it deep into His body, from where she had grabbed it lying against the wall.

"I didn't forget," Amy said. "I didn't forget to connect the earth . . ."

Flopping about, the doomed Tevas Endres was aging before her, centuries seeming to sweep across His face as He clawed for Amy, searching for her eyes. Unable to shake His dying gaze, Amy felt His very life rushing out of Him, His very strength fading, grounding out. Then she realized that their lives and strengths were still somehow together, this was not good, and He was trying to pull her into death with Him and she grabbed Him, lifting his shriveled, dying body—it weighed almost nothing now—and lifted it before her, shaking it, trying to get Him to release her before death seized Him.

"I surrender myself to you."

"What?"

"Your will be Mine. I am you. The birthright. You become Me."

"What? No . . ."

His dried, caked lips cracked and spoke one last time as the light from His eyes disappeared forever. "Remember me," he said quiet, very quiet now. A whisper. "Remember me . . ."

epilogue

PATIENCE, MASSACHUSETTS

Summer, 1999

She remembers everything, Amy does.

She's fifteen years old, always fifteen years old, and in Patience there is the first death and then the always death; the weight of it at first made her dizzy, the world rushing around her, because immortality would be one thing, but being fifteen forever is another, and never being able to leave Cyder Island something else again. . . .

Trapped. No new experiences, never able to see the world, or know it. Taste it. Remember it.

Except—there is a way, she knows it but fights it. For the longest time she fights it, not wanting to take anyone, make anyone go away, do any of the sending. She doesn't want to do it—what she had to do to Rat, Liz, the others, that was bad enough, but that was Him mostly, the last of His possession before His powers became hers, before she condemned Him away to silence forever, but most of all she didn't want to do it because she knew that eventually she would, eventually she *must*, because she isn't the same as everyone—anyone anymore.

'She took on the Greatest Mind in the World and made it hers. Hers. Wasn't she entitled?

Besides, how did a spider befriend the fly? How does the predator befriend the prey?

"I saw you yesterday."

"What?" Startled, she turned. There was a guy standing beside her now, interrupting her thoughts— the thoughts of the new Greatest Mind in the World. Such thoughtlessness. Still, at least he had been places, at least he wasn't doomed never to, of his volition, cross the waters, any moving waters.

"At the beach," he said. "You look at the ocean a lot, but you never go in."

"No." The guy was all tooth and goofy smile, but there was something false about it, as if it was forced goofiness, as if there was much more calculation to the smile. "Where are you from?"

"Here," She answered. "I'm an islander."

"An islander? Boring," he said. "You should come with me. I've been everywhere."

"Everywhere?"

"Yeah, my dad makes the big bucks. Takes me all over. I've been to France, Germany, Japan."

"Really?"

"Yeah. You want to get something to eat?"

"Sure," said Amy, realizing the best vacations are in the mind, anyone's mind but hers, except maybe there was a way around even that; perhaps this was something She was born for.

"Yeah," she said, the next generation immortal. "Let's go someplace where we can remember all of that together . . ."

Order Form

To order direct from the publishers, just make a list of the titles you want and fill in the form below:

Name ....

Address ....

....

....

Send to: Dept 6, HarperCollins Publishers Ltd, Westerhill Road, Bishopbriggs, Glasgow G64 2QT.

Please enclose a cheque or postal order to the value of the cover price, plus:

UK & BFPO: Add £1.00 for the first book, and 25p per copy for each addition book ordered.

Overseas and Eire: Add £2.95 service charge. Books will be sent by surface mail but quotes for airmail despatch will be given on request.

A 24-hour telephone ordering service is avail-able to Visa and Access card holders: 041-772 2281